Praise fo

"With *The Pole*, [J. M.] Coe[...]
national purity with his trade[...]
might read *The Pole* as a love story that unfolds across a
language barrier, it is at its heart a novel about language
that can be told only through a love plot. . . . The novel
presents words and what we desire to say as two points on
a map, as far apart as the poles. To confront the distance
between them is daunting, but love pushes us along."

—Jennifer Wilson, *The New Yorker*

"[A] masterclass in the 'late style' at its best. . . . [A]mong
the pleasures of *The Pole* are the layers it reveals. It is a
book not only of the living but also of the dead. What does
love mean? Coetzee wants us to consider. And memory—
what consolations can it offer when we know it doesn't
last? . . . In this deeply moving novel, Coetzee reminds us
of what we wish we didn't have to remember: that everything dissolves." —David L. Ulin, *Los Angeles Times*

"Like all of Mr. Coetzee's best books, *The Pole* is a textual
echo chamber—gesturing to Dante, *Don Quixote*, George
Sand and even Mr. Coetzee's own novel *Disgrace*—that never
feels smothered by its allusions. Quick, deft, stimulating,
stripped-down but unexpectedly moving, it's a return to
form by a writer who can make music from the fewest possible notes." —Sam Sacks, *Wall Street Journal*

"In *The Pole* [Coetzee] moves beyond rendering the opacity
of the beloved to suggest how love transforms the object
of its desire. In return, he displays renewed reverence to
the everyday ethical acts that, contrary to threatening the
survival of classics, secure their place in history."

—Jasmine Liu, *Los Angeles Review of Books*

"Haunting and surreptitiously heartfelt. . . . In an age of virtue signaling, Coetzee has the courage to bypass every fashionable position and reassurance and, by so doing, in *The Pole*, to catch some emotional truth, about loneliness and bewilderment and need, that really pierces. . . . [A]s soon as I completed it, I wanted to go back and read the whole elliptical thing again." —Pico Iyer, *Air Mail*

"*The Pole* shows that, at 83 years old, there is no diminishing of [Coetzee's] talents. Long may he darken our pages with prose." —John Self, *Guardian*

"Coetzee's prose is certainly economical. It avoids embellishment of any kind—adjectives, appositions, repetitions. . . . Its main purpose is to render the muddle and fog of experience with clarity and fluency, and in his later works Coetzee achieves this with the sprezzatura of an Old Master. There's not a sentence in *The Pole* that isn't crystal clear. And it flows with such grace that you could read it from beginning to end while standing propped up against the mantelpiece." —Nicholas Spice, *London Review of Books*

"In *The Pole*, Coetzee forges an autofiction of contemplation, in which thought and inquiry take precedence over melodrama—because time is running out." —Christian Lorentzen, *Financial Times*

"*The Pole* serves as an excellent microcosm of the human condition—scrutinizing, sharp, and delicate. . . . Contemplative and careful, this seemingly unassuming story will stick with the reader long after the last page is finished, as a stunning ending forces a reconsideration of all that preceded it." —Erlisa Demneri, *Harvard Crimson*

The
POLE

ALSO BY J. M. COETZEE

Life & Times of Michael K
Waiting for the Barbarians
In the Heart of the Country
Dusklands

NONFICTION

The Good Story: Exchanges on Truth, Fiction and Psycho-therapy (with Arabella Kurtz)
Here and Now: Letters 2008–2011 (with Paul Auster)
Inner Workings: Literary Essays 2000–2005
The Nobel Lecture in Literature, 2003
Stranger Shores: Literary Essays 1986–1999
Giving Offense: Essays on Censorship
Doubling the Point: Essays and Interviews
White Writing: On the Culture of Letters in South Africa

The
POLE

⇒ a novel ⇐

J. M. COETZEE

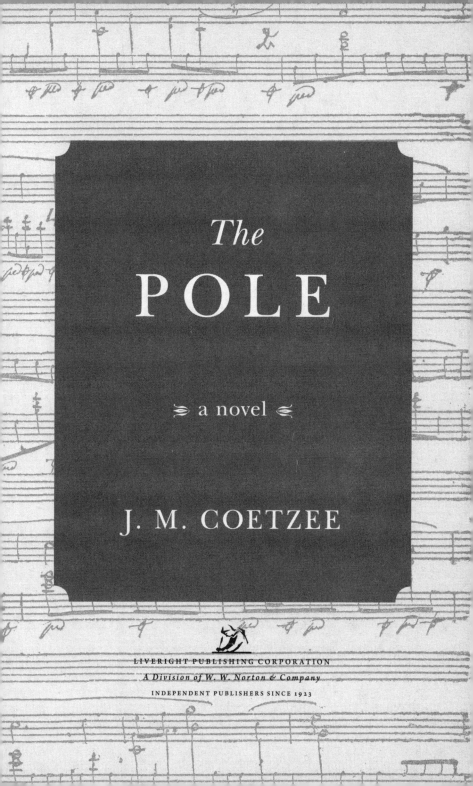

LIVERIGHT PUBLISHING CORPORATION

A Division of W. W. Norton & Company

INDEPENDENT PUBLISHERS SINCE 1923

The Pole was first published, in Spanish translation, as El Polaco (Buenos Aires: El Hilo de Ariadna, 2022).
Copyright © 2023, 2022 by J. M. Coetzee

All rights reserved
Printed in the United States of America
First printed as a Liveright paperback 2024

For information about permission to reproduce selections from this book, write to Permissions, Liveright Publishing Corporation, a division of W. W. Norton & Company, Inc., 500 Fifth Avenue, New York, NY 10110

For information about special discounts for bulk purchases, please contact W. W. Norton Special Sales at specialsales@wwnorton.com or 800-233-4830

Manufacturing by Lakeside Book Company
Book design by Beth Steidle
Production manager: Anna Oler

ISBN 978-1-324-09566-8 pbk.

Liveright Publishing Corporation
500 Fifth Avenue, New York, N.Y. 10110
www.wwnorton.com

W. W. Norton & Company Ltd.
15 Carlisle Street, London W1D 3BS

10 9 8 7 6 5 4 3 2 1

*My thanks to Maria Soledad Costantini,
Mariana Dimópulos, Georges Lory, and
Valerie Miles for counsel and advice
during the composition of* The Pole.

ONE

1. The woman is the first to give him trouble, followed soon afterwards by the man.

2. At the beginning he has a perfectly clear idea of who the woman is. She is tall and graceful; by conventional standards she may not qualify as a beauty but her features—dark hair and eyes, high cheekbones, full mouth—are striking and her voice, a low contralto, has a suave attractive power. Sexy? No, she is not sexy, and certainly not seductive. She might have been sexy when she was young—how can she not have been with a figure like that?—but now, in her forties, she goes in for a certain remoteness. She walks—one notices this particularly—without swinging her hips, gliding across the floor erect, even stately.

That is how he would sum up her exterior. As for her self, her soul, there is time for that to reveal itself. Of one thing he is convinced: she is a good person, kind, friendly.

3. The man is more troublesome. In concept, again, he is perfectly clear. He is a Pole, a man of seventy, a vigorous seventy, a concert pianist best known as an interpreter of Chopin, but a controversial interpreter: his Chopin is not at all Romantic but on the contrary somewhat austere, Chopin as inheritor of Bach. To that extent he is an oddity on the concert scene, odd enough to draw a small but discerning audience in Barcelona, the city to which he has been invited, the city where he will meet the graceful, soft-spoken woman.

But barely has the Pole emerged into the light than he begins to change. With his striking mane of silver hair, his idiosyncratic renderings of Chopin, the Pole promises to be a distinct enough personage. But in matters of soul, of feeling, he is troublingly opaque. At the piano he plays with soul, undeniably; but the soul that rules him is Chopin's, not his own. And if that soul strikes one as unusually dry and severe, it may point to a certain aridity in his own temperament.

4. Where do they come from, the tall Polish pianist and the elegant woman with the gliding walk, the banker's wife who occupies her days in good works? All year they have been knocking at the door, wanting to be let in or else dismissed and laid to rest. Now, at last, has their time come?

5. The invitation to the Pole comes from a Circle that stages monthly recitals in the Sala Mompou, in Barcelona's Gothic Quarter, and has been doing so for decades. The recitals are open to the public, but tickets are expensive and the audience tends to be wealthy, aging, and conservative in its tastes.

The woman in question—her name is Beatriz—is a member of the board that administers the series. She performs this role as a civic duty, but also because she believes that music is good in itself, as love is good, or charity, or beauty, and good furthermore in that it makes people better people. Though well aware that her beliefs are naive, she holds to them anyway. She is an intelligent person but not reflective. A portion of her intelligence consists in an awareness that excess of reflection can paralyse the will.

6. The decision to invite the Pole, whose name has so many w's and z's in it that no one on the board even tries to pronounce it—they refer to him simply as 'the Pole'—is arrived at only after some soul-searching. His candidacy was proposed not by her, Beatriz, but by her friend Margarita, the animating spirit behind the concert series, who in her youth studied at the conservatory in Madrid and knows much more about music than she does.

The Pole, says Margarita, led the way for a new generation of Chopin interpreters in his native land. She circulates a review of a concert he gave in London. According to the reviewer, the fashion for a hard, percussive Chopin—Chopin as Prokofiev—has had its day. It was never anything but a Modernist reaction against the branding of the Franco-Polish master as a delicate, dreamy, 'feminine' spirit. The emerging, historically authentic Chopin is soft-toned and Italianate. The Pole's revisionary reading of Chopin, even if somewhat over-intellectualized, is to be lauded.

She, Beatriz, is not sure that she wants to hear an evening's worth of historically authentic Chopin, nor, more pertinently, whether the rather staid Circle will take kindly to it. But Margarita feels strongly about the matter, and Margarita is her friend, so she gives her her support.

The invitation to the Pole accordingly went out, with a proposed date and a proposed fee, and was accepted. Now the day has arrived. He has flown in from Berlin, has been met at the airport and driven to his hotel. The plan for the evening is that, after the recital, she, together with Margarita and Margarita's husband, will take him out to dinner.

7. Why will Beatriz's own husband not be one of the party? The answer: because he never attends Concert Circle events.

8. The plan is simple enough. But then there is a hitch. On the morning in question Margarita telephones to say that she has fallen ill. That is the rather formal term she uses: *caído enferma*, fallen ill. What has she fallen ill with? She does not say. She is vague, deliberately so, it would seem. But she will not be coming to the recital. Nor will her husband. Therefore will she, Beatriz, please take over the duties of hospitality, that is to say, arrange to have their guest conveyed from hotel to auditorium in good time, and entertain him afterwards, if he wants to be entertained, so that when he returns to his native country he will be able to say to his friends, *Yes, I had a good time in Barcelona, on the whole. Yes, they took good care of me.*

'Very well,' says Beatriz, 'I will do it. And I hope you get better soon.'

9. She has known Margarita since they were children together at the nuns' school; she has always admired her friend's spirit, her enterprise, her social aplomb. Now she must take her place. What will it entail, entertaining a man on a fleeting visit to a strange city? Surely, at his age, he will not expect sex. But he will certainly expect

to be flattered, even flirted with. Flirting is not an art she has ever cared to master. Margarita is different. Margarita has a light touch with men. She, Beatriz, has more than once, with amusement, watched her friend go about her conquests. But she has no wish to imitate her. If their guest has high expectations in the department of flattery, he is going to be disappointed.

10. The Pole is, according to Margarita, a 'truly memorable' pianist. She heard him in the flesh, in Paris. Is it possible that something happened between the two of them, Margarita and the Pole, in the flesh; and that, having engineered his visit to Barcelona, Margarita is at the last minute having cold feet? Or has her husband finally had enough, and issued a fiat? Is that how 'falling ill' is to be understood? Why must everything be so complicated!

And now she must take care of the stranger! There is no reason to expect he speaks Spanish. What if he does not speak English either? What if he is the kind of Pole who speaks French? The only regulars in the Concert Circle who speak French are the Lesinskis, Ester and Tomás; and Tomás, in his eighties, is becoming infirm.

How will the Pole feel when, instead of the vivacious Margarita, he is offered the decrepit Lesinskis?

She is not looking forward to the evening. What a life, she thinks, the life of an itinerant entertainer! The airports, the hotels, all different yet all the same; the hosts to put up with, all different yet all the same: gushing middle-aged women with bored attendant husbands. Enough to quench whatever spark there is in the soul.

At least she does not gush. Nor does she chatter. If after his performance the Pole wants to retreat into moody silence, she will be moody right back.

11. Producing a concert, making sure that everything runs smoothly, is no small feat. The burden has now fallen squarely on her. She spends the afternoon at the concert hall, chivvying the staff (their supervisor is, in her experience, dilatory), ticking off details. Is it necessary to list the details? No. But it is by her attention to detail that Beatriz will prove that she possesses the virtues of diligence and competence. By comparison, the Pole will show himself to be impractical, unenterprising. If one can conceive of virtue as a quantity, then the greater part of the Pole's virtue is spent on his music, leaving hardly any behind for his dealings with the world; whereas Beatriz's virtue is expended evenly in all directions.

12. Publicity photographs show a man with a craggy profile and a shock of white hair staring into the middle distance. The accompanying biography says that Witold Walczykiewicz was born in 1943 and made his concert debut at the age of fourteen. It lists prizes he has won and some of his recordings.

She wonders what it was like to be born in 1943, in Poland, in the middle of a war, with nothing to eat but cabbage-and-potato-peel soup. Is one's physical development stunted? And what of the spirit? Will Witold W prove to bear, in his bones, in his spirit, the marks of a starved childhood?

A baby wailing in the night, wailing with hunger.

She was born in 1967. In 1967 no one in Europe had to eat cabbage soup: no one in Poland, no one in Spain. She has never known hunger. Never. A blessed generation.

Her sons too have been blessed. They have turned out to be energetic young men deeply involved in independent projects of making successes of their lives. If they ever wailed in the night, it was because of nappy rash, or out of simple petulance, not because they were starving.

In their drive for success, her sons take after their father, not their mother. Their father has made an indubitable success of his life. As for their mother, one cannot yet be sure. Is it enough to have propelled two such well-fed, energetic young male beings into the world?

13. She is an intelligent person, well educated, well read, a good wife and mother. But she is not taken seriously. Nor is Margarita. Nor is the rest of their Circle. Society ladies: it is not difficult to make fun of them. Mocked for their good works. Mocked by themselves too. What a risible fate! Would she ever have guessed that it awaited her?

Perhaps that is why Margarita has chosen to fall ill today of all days. *¡Basta!* Enough of good works!

14. Her own husband keeps his distance from the Concert Circle. He believes in separate spheres of activity. A wife's sphere of activities should be her own.

They have grown apart, she and her husband. They were students together; he was her first love. In those early days they had a great passion for each other, insatiable. That passion persisted even after the birth of the children. Then one day it was no longer there. He had had enough. She too. Nonetheless she has remained a faithful wife. Men make passes at her, which she evades, not because they are unwelcome but because she has not taken the step yet, the step that is hers alone to take, the step from No to Yes.

15. She has her first sight of the Pole, in the flesh, when he strides onto the platform, takes a bow, and seats himself at the Steinway.

Born in 1943, therefore seventy-two years old. He moves easily; he does not look his age.

She is struck by how tall he is. Not just tall but big too, with a chest that seems about to burst out of his jacket. Crouched over the keyboard, he looks like a huge spider.

Hard to imagine great hands like that coaxing anything sweet and gentle out of a keyboard. Yet they do.

Do male pianists have an inborn advantage over women: hands that on a woman would look grotesque?

She has not given much thought to hands before, hands that do everything for their owners like obedient, unpaid servants. Her own hands are nothing special. The hands of a woman who will soon be fifty. Sometimes she discreetly hides them. Hands betray one's age, as does one's throat, as do the folds of one's armpit.

In her mother's day, a woman could still appear in public wearing gloves. Gloves, hats, veils: last traces of a vanished epoch.

16. The second thing that strikes her about the Pole is his hair, which is extravagantly white, extravagantly waved in a crest. Is that how he prepares for a recital, she wonders: seated with a hairdresser in his hotel room having his coiffure attended to? But perhaps she is ungenerous. Among maestros of his generation, the heirs of the Abbé Liszt, a mane of hair, grey or white, must be standard equipment.

Years later, when the episode of the Pole has receded into history, she will wonder about those early impressions. She believes, on the whole, in first impressions, when the heart delivers its verdict, either reaching out to the stranger or recoiling from him. Her heart did not reach out to the Pole when she saw him stride onto the platform, toss back his mane, and address the keyboard. Her heart's verdict: *What a poseur! What an old clown!* It would take her a while to overcome that first, instinctive response, to see the Pole in his full selfhood. But what does *full selfhood* mean, really? Did the Pole's full selfhood not perhaps include being a poseur, an old clown?

17. The evening's recital falls into two halves. The first half consists of a Haydn sonata and a suite of dances by Lutosławski. The second half is given over to Chopin's twenty-four Preludes.

He plays the Haydn sonata with clean, crisp lines, as if to demonstrate that big hands need not be clumsy hands, but on the contrary can dance together as delicately as a lady's.

The little pieces by Lutosławski are new to her. They remind her of Bartók, of his peasant dances. She likes them.

She likes them more than the Chopin that follows. The Pole may have made a name as an interpreter of Chopin, but the Chopin she knows is more intimate and more subtle than what he offers. Her Chopin has the power to transport her out of the Barri Gòtic, out of Barcelona, into the drawing room of a great old country house in the remote Polish plains, with a long summer's day wheeling to an end, a breeze stirring the curtains, and the scent of roses wafting indoors.

To be transported, to be lost in transports: an outdated idea, in all likelihood, of what music does for its listeners—outdated and probably sentimental too. But that is what she desires on this particular evening, and that is what the Pole does not provide.

The applause, after the last of the Preludes, is polite but not enthusiastic. She is not the only one who came to hear Chopin played by a real Pole, and has been disappointed.

As an encore, as a gesture to his hosts, he offers a short piece by Mompou, played in a rather abstracted way, then with nary a smile is gone from the stage.

Does he happen to be in a bad mood today or is he always like this? Is he going to call home and complain about his reception at the hands of the philistine Catalans? Is there a Madame Pole back at home to hear his complaints? He does not look like a married man. He looks like a man with messy divorces behind him, and ex-wives grinding their teeth, wishing him ill.

18. The Pole, it turns out, does not speak French. He does, however, speak English, after a fashion; as for her, Beatriz, after her two years at Mount Holyoke she is fluent in the language. The polyglot Lesinskis are therefore supernumerary. But welcome nonetheless, taking some of the hostly burden off her shoulders. Ester in particular. Ester may be old and bent, but she is as sharp as a pin.

19. They take him to the restaurant to which they routinely take performers, an Italian establishment called Boffini's with too much bottle-green velvet in its decor but with a dependable Milanese chef.

Once they are seated, Ester is the first to speak. 'It must be difficult, maestro, to come to earth after you have been in the clouds with your sublime music.'

The Pole inclines his head, neither agreeing nor disagreeing about the clouds where he has been. At close quarters it is less easy to conceal marks of age. There are pouches under his eyes; the skin of his throat sags; the backs of his hands are mottled.

Maestro. Best to get it over with quickly, the question of names. 'If I may,' she says: 'how shall we address you? We in Spain find Polish names difficult, as you must have realized by now. And we can't go on calling you *maestro* all evening.'

'My name is Witold,' he says. 'You can call me Witold. Please.'

'And I am Beatriz. Our friends are Ester and Tomás.'

The Pole raises an empty glass to his three new friends: Ester, Tomás, Beatriz.

'I am sure, Witold,' says Ester, 'I am not the first to confuse you with that famous Swedish actor, you must know whom I mean.'

The ghost of a smile crosses the Pole's face. 'Max von Sydow,' he says. 'My bad brother. He follows me wherever I go.'

Ester is right: the same long, lugubrious face, the same faded blue eyes, the same erect posture. But the voice is disappointing. It lacks the bad brother's deep-throated resonance.

20. 'Tell us about Poland, Witold,' says Ester. 'Tell us why your countryman Frédéric Chopin chose to live in France rather than in his homeland.'

'If Chopin had lived longer he would have returned to Poland,' replies the Pole, managing the tenses warily but correctly. 'He was a young man when he departed, he was a young man when he died. Young men are not happy at home. They search adventure.'

'And you?' says Ester. 'Were you, like him, unhappy in your home country when you were a young man?'

It is an opportunity for the Pole, Witold, to tell them about what it was like to be young and restless in his unhappy homeland, about his yearning to escape to the decadent but exciting West, but he does not take it. 'Happiness is not the most important . . . the most important sentiment,' he says. 'Anyone can be happy.'

Anyone can be happy but it takes someone extraordinary to be unhappy, someone extraordinary like me—is that what he wants them to infer? She hears herself speak. 'What then is the most important sentiment, Witold? If happiness is not important, what is important?'

There is silence around the table. She catches Ester and her husband in a quick exchange of glances. *Is she going to make things difficult? These difficult hours that stretch before us—is she going to make them even more difficult?*

'I am a musician,' says the Pole. 'For me music is most important.'

He is not answering her question, he is deflecting it, but no matter. What she would like to ask, but does not, is: *What of Madame Witold? How does she feel when her husband says that happiness is not important? Or is there no Madame—did Madame run away long ago to find happiness in another's arms?*

21. He does not speak of Madame Witold but does speak of a daughter who had a training in music, then moved to Germany to sing in a band and did not come back. 'I went to hear her once. In Düsseldorf. It was good. She has a good voice. Good voice, good control, not so good music.'

'Yes, the young . . .' says Ester. 'They bring us such heartache. Still, it must be nice for you—nice to know that the musical line is being continued. And your country—how are affairs in your country nowadays? I remember the good Pope, he was from there, was he not? John Paul.'

On the subject of John Paul the good Pope, the Pole

seems reluctant to be drawn. She, Beatriz, does not regard John Paul as a good pope. Not even as a good man. He struck her from the beginning as a schemer, a politician.

22. They speak of the young Japanese violinist who was last month's visitor. 'Extraordinary technique,' says Tomás. 'It commences very early in Japan, the education for music. Two years old, three years old, the child carries a violin with him everywhere. To the toilet too! It is part of the body, like another arm, arm number three. At what age did you commence, maestro?'

'My mother was a singer,' says the Pole, 'so always in the house I was hearing music. My mother was my first teacher. Then another teacher, then to the academy in Kraków.'

'So you have always been a pianist. From a child.'

Gravely the Pole considers the word *pianist*. 'I have been a man who plays piano,' he says at last. 'Like the man who punches tickets in the bus. He is a man and he punches tickets, but he is not a ticket man.'

So in Poland, in the buses, they still have men who punch tickets—they have not been rationalized away. Maybe that is why young Witold did not run away to

Paris, like his musical hero. Because in Poland they have men who punch tickets and men who play the piano. For the first time she warms to him. *Behind that solemn air,* she thinks to herself, *he may just possibly be a joker. Just possibly.*

23. 'You should try the veal,' says Tomás. 'The veal is always good here.'

The Pole demurs. 'In the evening I do not have a big stomach,' he says. He orders a salad followed by gnocchi with pesto.

A big stomach: might that be a Polish idiom? He certainly does not have a big stomach. He is even a bit—she reaches for a word she does not often have a need for—*cadavérico*, cadaverous. A man like that should bequeath his body to a medical school. They would appreciate having such big bones to practise their skills on.

Chopin was buried in Paris, but then afterwards, if she remembers correctly, some patriotic organization or other had him exhumed and transported back to the land of his birth. A tiny body, no weight at all. Tiny bones. Is such a tiny man big enough, great enough, to devote one's whole life to—a dreamer, when all is said and done, a weaver of elegant sonic fabrics? A serious question, to her mind.

Compared to Chopin, compared even to Witold his disciple, she does not of course count as a serious person. She knows that and accepts it. But surely she is entitled to know whether the hours she spends listening patiently to the tinkling of piano keys or the scraping of horsehair on gut, when she could be out on the streets feeding the poor, are not hours wasted but form part of a grander, richer design. *Speak!* she wants to say to the Pole. *Justify your art!*

24. Of course the man has no idea of what is going on inside her. To him she is part of the burden he has to bear for the sake of his career as a performer: one of those nagging wealthy women who will not leave him in peace until they have extorted their gram of flesh. At this very moment, in his correct but slow English, he is relating a story of the kind he presumes a woman like her wants to hear, a story about his first piano teacher, who sat over him with a *férula* and rapped him on the wrist whenever he made a mistake.

25. 'And now you must reveal to us, Witold,' says Ester: 'of all the cities of the world that you visit, which

are you fondest of? Where—outside Barcelona, of course—do you get the warmest reception?'

Without allowing the Pole his chance to reply, to reveal which of the cities of the world is his favourite, she, Beatriz, cuts in. 'Before you tell us that, Witold, can we for a moment go back to Chopin? Why does Chopin live on, do you think? Why is he so important?'

The Pole inspects her coolly. 'Why is he important? Because he tells us about ourselves. About our desires. Which are sometimes not clear to us. That is my opinion. Which are sometimes desires for that which we cannot have. That which is beyond us.'

'I don't understand.'

'You do not understand because I do not explain well in English, not in any language, even in Polish. To understand you must be silent and listen. Let the music speak, then you will understand.'

She is not satisfied. The fact is, she listened this evening, listened intently, and did not like what she heard. If the Lesinskis were not there, if she were alone with the man, she would press him harder. *It is not Chopin who fails to speak to me, Witold, but* your *Chopin, the Chopin who uses* you *as his medium*—that is what she would say. *Claudio Arrau—you know him?—*she would go on—

Arrau remains, for me, a better interpreter, a better medium. Through Arrau, Chopin speaks to my heart. But of course Arrau was not from Poland, so perhaps there was something he was deaf to, some feature of the mystery of Chopin that foreigners will never understand.

26. The evening has run its course. On the sidewalk outside Boffini's the Lesinskis take their leave ('Such a privilege, maestro!'). It is left to her to conduct the Pole back to his hotel.

Side by side in the taxi, talked out, they sit in silence. *What a day!* she thinks. She cannot wait to get into bed.

She is all too conscious of his smell, the smell of male sweat and eau de Cologne. Of course it is always hot on the platform under the lights. And the effort, the physical effort, of hitting all those keys, one after the other, in the correct order! So perhaps the smell can be excused. But still . . .

They arrive at the hotel. 'Good night, gracious lady,' says the Pole. He takes her hand and squeezes it. 'Thank you. Thank you too for your profound questions. I will not forget.' Then he is gone.

She inspects her hand. After its brief rest under that giant paw it seems smaller than usual. But unharmed.

27. A week after his departure a package arrives at the concert hall, addressed to her, with German postage stamps. It contains a CD—his recording of the Chopin Nocturnes—and a note in English: 'To the angel who watched over me in Barcelona. I pray that the music will speak to her. Witold.'

28. Does she like this man, Witold? Perhaps she does, on balance. She is sorry, mildly sorry, that she will not see him again. She likes the way he stands straight, sits up straight. She likes his attentiveness, the seriousness with which he listens to her when she speaks. *The woman with the profound questions*: she is glad he acknowledged that. And she is amused by his English, with its correct grammar and faulty idioms. What does she dislike about him? A number of things. Above all his dentures, too gleaming, too white, too fake.

TWO

1. She sleeps well that night. In the morning she plunges back into her routines. She promises herself she will find time to listen to the Pole's CD, but then forgets.

Months later an email pops up. How did he get her address? 'Esteemed lady, I am teaching master classes in Girona at the Conservatori Felip Pedrell. Your hospitality is not forgotten. May I offer you hospitality? If you will come to Girona I will be your host with pleasure. I will meet the train at any hour.' It is signed *Your friend Witold with the difficult name.*

She writes back. 'Dear Witold, Your friends in Barcelona remember your visit with pleasure. Thank you for the kind invitation. Unfortunately I am too busy at present to come to Girona. I wish you every success with your classes. Beatriz.'

She makes inquiries. What the man with the difficult name says is true: he is indeed giving piano classes in Girona. Why Girona, of all places? Surely he does not need the money.

The more she thinks about his return to Catalonia, the stranger it seems.

She writes a second email. 'Why are you here, Witold? Please be frank with me. I have no time for pretty lies. Beatriz.'

She deletes *I have no time for pretty lies* and sends the message. It is not just lies that she has no time for, but also circumlocutions, word games, veiled meanings.

His reply comes at once. 'I am here for you. I do not forget you.'

2. She allows a day to pass while she ruminates on *for you*. Whatever the words mean in English, whatever they mean in the Polish that presumably lies behind the English, what do they mean in reality? He is here for her

as one is in a bakery for bread? And what does *here* mean anyway? What good does it do him if his *here* is Girona while hers is Barcelona? Or he is here for her as one is in a church for God?

3. When she was young she would unquestioningly follow impulses. She trusted her heart. *Yes*, said her heart. Or *No*. But (thank God!) she is no longer young. She is wiser, more prudent. She sees things as they are.

What does she see in the case of the Pole? She sees a man at the end of his career, driven by need or circumstance to take on a job that would once have been beneath him (the Conservatori Felip Pedrell is not a highly regarded institution), a man who, finding himself alone and lonely in a foreign town, makes a play for a woman he once crossed paths with. What would it say about her if she were to respond? More to the point, what does it say about her that the man expects she will respond?

4. Apart from her husband, she has no deep experience of men. But over the years she has given ear to

numerous confessions and confidences from women friends. She has also with a cool eye observed how the men of her class behave. She has emerged from her explorations with no great respect for men and their appetites, no wish to have a wave of male passion splash over her.

She has never been a great traveller. Her husband finds her incurious. He is wrong. She is curious, deeply curious. But not about the wider world, and not about sex. What then is she curious about? About herself. About why, despite all, the thought of driving to Girona for the day tickles her fancy, makes her smile.

5. Without difficulty she finds her way to the Conservatori, a faceless building in the old part of the city. Its corridors are empty (it is early afternoon). Following a familiar melody, she opens a door marked Sala 1 and finds herself at the rear of a small auditorium. On the stage, at the piano, are the Pole and a young man. Noiselessly she slips into a seat. The students who make up the audience, thirty or so of them, pay her no attention.

They are working on the slow movement of Rachmaninov's second piano concerto. The young man embarks on the long, plaintive opening melody. The Pole lays a hand on his arm to halt him. 'La—la—la—la—la—la—la—*laa*,' he sings, prolonging the final *la*. '*No demasiado legato.*'

The young man tries the melody again, with less *legato*.

Wearing slacks and an open-neck shirt, the Pole looks more relaxed than she remembers him. *Good!* she thinks. *And he has picked up a few words of Spanish!* Though to teach music one does not need many words. *Sí. No.*

She has not heard him sing before. An unexpectedly deep voice, like a dark stream, liquid.

6. What interests her about the scene is not the music but the drama. Because they are on a stage, because there is an audience, teacher and pupil have perforce become actors. How does the young man respond to direction when perhaps he does not agree with it (perhaps his way of playing, with more *legato*, was close to his heart)? Does he submit or does he rebel? Or does he pretend to submit but secretly rebel, promising himself

he will go back to the old way once the Pole has vanished from the scene? And what of the Pole? Does he play the role of autocrat or of fatherly adviser?

7. The Pole leans over and plays the broken chords that open the movement. In the voice of the clarinet, he sings: 'La—la—la—la—la—la—la—*laa*.' Then the right hand enters, and at once she hears the difference. Less *legato*, less emotion, more tension, more lift.

The young man follows, and this time gets it right. He is good. He learns quickly. The Pole nods. '*Continúe.*'

8. The lesson ends, the students drift away. She stays behind. The Pole approaches her. What will he say?

He takes her hand. He thanks her, in English, for coming. He expresses his pleasure at seeing her again. He compliments her on the dress she is wearing. His compliments do not please her. They have a practised, rehearsed air. But perhaps he simply does not know how to sound easy in English. Perhaps back in Poland he is a perfectly charming gentleman.

She has dressed carefully for the occasion. That is to say, she has dressed soberly.

'Can we talk?' she says.

9. They go for a walk on a tree-lined path along the riverside. It is a pleasant autumn day. The leaves are turning, et cetera.

'I ask again,' she says: 'why have you come here? Girona—you have no reason to be in Girona.'

'We all have to be somewhere. We cannot be nowhere. That is the human condition. But no. I am here for you.'

'So you say, but what does it mean? What do you want from me? You did not invite me here to listen to your piano classes. Do you want me to sleep with you? If so, let me tell you at once: it is not going to happen.'

'Do not be angry,' he says. 'Please.'

'I am not angry. I am impatient. I don't have time for games. You invited me here. Why?'

Why is she so angry? What does she want from him that he is refusing to give?

'Dear lady,' says the Pole, 'you remember Dante

Alighieri the poet? His Beatrice never gave him one word and he loved her all his life.'

Dear lady!

'And is that why I am here: to be informed that you plan to love me all your life?'

'My life is not so long,' says the Pole.

Poor fool! she wants to say. *You come too late, the feast is over.*

She shakes her head. 'We are strangers, you and I,' she says. 'We belong to different worlds, different realms. You belong in one world with your Dante and your Beatrice, I belong in another, which I am accustomed to call the real world.'

'You give me peace,' says the Pole. 'You are my symbol of peace.'

She, Beatriz, a symbol of peace! She has never heard anything more nonsensical.

10. They walk on. The river flows softly, a breeze blows, the footpath stretches before them. Details, incidental yet not unimportant. Step by step her mood lightens.

'When you were teaching your student you sang,' she says. 'I had never thought of you as a singer. You have a good voice.'

'From my mother I am a singer. From my mother I am a musician.'

A mother's boy. Is that what he is in quest of: mothering?

Time is getting short. Either he must begin to plead his cause or she will get in her car and drive home and that will be the end of it. It is time for his grand aria. He must sing: that is her demand. In Italian, in Spanish, in English, it does not matter which. Even in Polish.

'Dear lady,' says the Pole, 'I am not a poet. I can only say, since I met you my memory is full of you, the image of you. I travel from one city to another city to another city, that is my job, but always you are with me. You protect me. I have peace inside me. I say to myself, I must find her, she is my destiny. Therefore I am here. And with such joy to see you!'

She gives him peace. She gives him joy. Not much of an aria. Also, his destiny has been revealed to him, and she is it. But what about her? Does she not have a destiny too? What might that destiny be? When will it be revealed?

11. She has no reason to disbelieve him when he says that because of her, because of a chance invitation that brought him to Barcelona, he now has intervals of peace and joy. He bears her image with him as a lover in the old days bore the image of his sweetheart in a locket around his neck. Very pretty. If she were young, if he were young, she might be flattered. But from a man born in 1943, a man old enough to be her father, the bid he is making for her is neither amusing nor flattering. It is, if anything, distasteful.

'Listen to me, Witold,' she says. 'You barely know me, so let me tell you who I am. First and last, I am a married woman. Not a free spirit but a woman with a husband and children and a home and friends and commitments of all kinds, emotional commitments, social commitments, practical commitments. There is no room in my life for—what shall I call it?—an affair of the heart. You tell me you carry around with you an image of me. Good. But I don't carry around an image of you. I don't carry around an image of anyone. I am not that kind of person. You visited Barcelona, you gave a piano recital, which we all enjoyed; we had dinner together; and that was that. You passed into my life, you passed out of my life. *Terminado*. We have no future together, you and I. I am sorry to say so, but it is the truth. Now I think we should turn back. It is getting late.'

12. 'I will make a proposal,' says the Pole.

They are sitting in a café across the street from where her car is parked.

'Next month I go on a tour to America. After America I go to Brazil. I have three concerts there. Do you know Brazil? No? Perhaps you will come to Brazil with me.'

'You want me to come to Brazil?'

'Yes. We will have a vacation. Do you like the sea? We can have our vacation next to the sea.'

She likes the sea, likes it very much. She is a good swimmer, strong in the water, like a seal. Strong and agile. But that is not the question.

'And what shall I say to my husband?' she says. 'That I am going off to Brazil with a man I barely know? And you? What do you plan to say to your wife? You have never told me—are you married?'

He sets down his cup; his hand quivers noticeably. Does she make him nervous? Is he about to tell a lie?

'No, I am not married. Once I was married, but now, no. Say to your husband the truth. The truth is always good. He is a man of affairs. He is free, you are free.'

'You astonish me. You know nothing about my husband. My husband is not "a man of affairs." Nor am I a woman of affairs. And let me tell you, for use in the future, this is not how a man goes about luring a woman into going off to Brazil with him. Perhaps it works in Poland, but not here. I must go now. I have a long drive ahead of me.'

She rises. It is the Pole's last chance. He too rises, to his full and considerable height, grips her by the shoulders. The people at the next table glance across: are they going to witness a domestic quarrel? She pulls free of his grasp. 'I really must go.'

13. On the highway, near the turnoff to Malgrat, she passes a crash site: a tangle of metal, police cars, an ambulance. She shivers. *What if that had been me? What would people say? 'What was she doing in Girona?'*

What was she doing in Girona indeed? Already it seems like an aberration: answering the call of a man whose name she cannot spell. Answering his call, but then recovering herself, thank God! *Come with me to Brazil.* What nonsense!

14. She speaks to her husband. 'I don't know if you remember, but some months ago we had a pianist from Poland at the Concert Circle. It turns out he is now in Girona, giving classes at the conservatorium. He invited me there.'

'Yes? And you will go?'

'I was there this afternoon. He wants me to come with him to Brazil. He has fallen in love with me. So he says.'

'And will you go?'

'Of course not. I am just telling you.'

Why is she telling him? So that she can draw a line under the story. So that her conscience can be clean.

'Are you jealous?' she says.

'Of course I am jealous. I would be jealous of any man who fell in love with you.'

But he is not jealous. She can see that. He is, if anything, amused: amused that another man should aspire to what belongs to him alone, to what he owns so easily.

'Will you see him again?' says her husband.

'No,' she says. And then: 'It is not about sex.'

'Of course it is about sex. Why else do you think he has invited you to Brazil? To sit by his side and turn the pages of his piano score?'

15. From the Pole arrives a long letter, whose surface she skims. Peace seems to be the key word. She brings him peace. Peace as opposed to what? War? What does he know about war, sitting in front of a piano all day, lost in the clouds?

Ahead of her she catches a glimpse of the B word, *Brazil.* Without reading further, she deletes the letter.

16. She is incurious about her husband's affairs, deliberately so. In return, he is careful not to involve himself with women from their own social circle. That is the modus vivendi they have arrived at, and it has served them well.

17. Another email from the Pole. Today is his last day in Girona, he will be passing through Barcelona tomorrow on his way to the airport for a flight to Berlin. Will

she have lunch with him? 'Sorry, no time,' she writes back. 'Travel safely. Beatriz.'

18. She resurrects the CD he sent her, brings home the Walczykiewicz CDs from the Concert Circle's little library, and listens to them in solitude. Why? Because she is prepared to entertain the idea that what the man cannot express in his bare-bones English he may be able to express through his art.

She starts with the Nocturnes. What was Chopin saying to the world when he dreamed up his Nocturnes? More important, what was the Pole saying to the world on the day he made the recording? Most important of all, what might the Pole, on the day he made the recording, have been revealing of himself to a woman of whose existence in the real world he had as yet no inkling?

As before, she is disappointed. She finds herself chilled by—what shall she call it?—the style, the approach, the mentality of the interpreter. So dry, so matter-of-fact! Each piece held up for inspection, examined, then, with the final chord, folded away and interred.

Perhaps the truth is that, even at the time when he made the recording (she checks the notes on the CD:

2009, they say), the Pole was too old in spirit for music like this, music that belongs to more ardent souls.

Something to do with touch. She recalls the touch of his hand in the taxi on the evening they met; she recalls the touch of his lips to her cheek when he greeted her in Girona. Like being touched by dry bone. A living skeleton. She shivers. She too has a skeleton, but unlike his hers is ghostly, impalpable.

Is that, then, her final verdict on him: too dry, too lacking in ardour? Is that what she wants in a man: ardour? If ardour were to arrive tomorrow, out of the blue, and announce itself—real, impetuous ardour— would there be room for it in her life? She doubts it.

19. Of all the music he has recorded, it is the mazur-kas that she likes best. He comes most alive when he joins his master in these country dances. Strange: she does not think of him as a dancer.

20. Perhaps, after all, the fault does not lie wholly with the Pole, the two Poles—the young one long dead, the old one still current. Perhaps she carries a share of

the blame. All that she seems to like in music nowadays is song and dance, not drama with its ups and downs (*forte! piano! forte! piano!*) and certainly not philoso-phizing. Music that spends its time questing after a lost object (Mahler) makes her yawn. That is why the Pole himself does not interest her, in the end. Roaming the world in search of his own lost object, he has chanced upon her, Beatriz, and turned her into a fetish. *You bring me peace*: what nonsense! *I am not the answer to the riddle of your life, Señor Witold—your riddle or anyone else's!* That is what she should have said to him. *I am who I am!*

21. For years she and her husband have not shared a bedroom. The arrangement suits them both. She likes to go to bed early after a hot bath, whereas he likes to stay up late. She sleeps better alone, and so perhaps does he. She sleeps eight hours a night, sometimes nine. She sleeps deeply, nourishingly.

She and her husband are no longer intimate. She is getting used to doing without sex. She does not seem to need it. Her climacteric has not yet arrived, but is on its way. Then she will cease to be fruitful, and the body's faint cry for union will die away.

22. Her friends have love affairs but she does not. Her friend Margarita is having an affair with a well-known professor of anthropology, a media celebrity, a married man. They meet in hotels or in an apartment belonging to an obliging colleague.

23. She has visited Argentina but never Brazil. She would not mind seeing Brazil. It seems an interesting country. Perhaps her elder son, who works as a chemist for an agronomics company, would find it useful to accompany her there. He could explore Brazilian agriculture.

24. She has no intention of going to Brazil in the company of the Polish pianist. Anyway, if she were to go, how would he explain her to his Brazilian hosts—to the Brazilian equivalent of her Concert Circle? 'This is Beatriz, an old friend from the city of Barcelona, who is accompanying me on my tour. Beatriz has long wanted to see your infinitely various country.' Or: 'This is Beatriz, whom I have brought with me to soothe my brow and give me

peace.' Or: 'This is Beatriz, a woman I barely know but who seems to be the answer to the riddle of why I exist.'

25. An old man in love. Foolish. And a danger to himself.

26. He had his chance when he gripped her by the shoulders in the café in Girona and thrust his face at her, his cold blue eyes. That was the moment for him to make his mark on her, to overbear her resistance. But he faltered and lost her.

27. She dislikes the Portuguese language, with its tight, choked sounds. But perhaps the Portuguese spoken in Brazil is different.

28. She thinks of how it would be to share a bed with that huge bony frame, and shivers with distaste. Those cold hands on her body.

29. Why her? What happened, during the evening they spent over dinner at Boffini's, that made him think, *This is my destiny! This is a woman on whom I must spend my last love?* If Margarita had not been ill that day but had been one of the party, would he have fallen for Margarita instead, and would Margarita now be the one invited to Brazil to soothe his brow and share his bed?

Peace: that is what he says he wants. As a storm-tossed navigator prays for landfall, so he prays for peace. Well, Margarita is no angel of peace, as he would soon discover. Margarita would fit him out with new, more modish clothes, take him to her *esteticista* to have his eyebrows attended to, fix him up with media interviews. As for sex, would he, at his age, be able to perform to Margarita's demanding standard?

Perhaps, if the truth be told, that is why he settled on her, Beatriz. Because in his line of work he comes across too many women like Margarita, energetic, brilliant, acquisitive; because, that evening at Boffini's, she, Beatriz, seemed the epitome of the unobtrusive, undemanding yet entirely presentable woman who would attend to his needs without giving too much trouble. If so, what an insult!

30. She writes a letter to him, in English: 'Dear Witold, I trust that your concert in Berlin went well. I have been reflecting on our last conversation, wondering how on earth you came to the conclusion that I am the embodiment of peace. I embody neither peace nor anything else. The fact is, you know nothing of who or what I am. Your path crossed mine by the purest of chance. There was no design behind it. I was not meant for you, as you seem to think. I was not "meant" for anyone. None of us is "meant," whatever the word means. Yours, Beatriz.'

31. Between a man and a woman, between the two poles, electricity either crackles or does not crackle. So it has been since the beginning of time. A man *and* a woman, not just a man, a woman. Without *and* there is no conjunction. Between herself and the Pole there is no *and*.

Next month's visitor to the Concert Circle will be the counter-tenor Thomas Kirchwey, who will present a program of Handel, Pergolesi, Philip Glass, and someone named Martynov whom she has never heard of. Perhaps Thomas Kirchwey will turn out to be her true pole, eclipsing the false Pole, the pretender.

32. She rereads her letter, decides that it sounds too angry, deletes it. Why does it sound angry? She did not feel angry when she wrote it.

33. His idol Chopin was a sickly man who relied on a woman to look after him. Perhaps that is what the Pole really wants: a nurse to take care of him in his declining years.

34. 'That pianist you told me about, the one with the long name,' says her husband—'have you made up your mind yet?'

'Made up my mind about what?'

'Will you be going with him to Brazil?'

'Of course not. Whatever made you think I would?'

'Does he know you will not be coming with him?'

'Of course he does. I made it clear to him.'

'Does he call you? Does he write to you? Are you and he in correspondence?'

'In correspondence? No, we are not. And I am not answering any more questions. Don't you find this a strange conversation for the two of us to be having—a civilized married couple?'

35. Now there are two puzzles to solve: why her mind keeps going back to the Pole; and why her husband has turned hostile.

The second is the easier to answer. Her husband has sniffed something in the air and is reacting. It is a matter of psychology, nothing more.

The first is not a matter of psychology. It is a matter of missing things, and for missing things there seems to be, as yet, no ology. Mysterology? Mysterics?

36. Two images of Brazil come to her mind's eye, two stereotypes: bronzed bodies lazing on beaches of dazzling whiteness; and women with wailing babies sweating over gas stoves in leaky shacks. Of course that is not

all of Brazil. A third Brazil, a fourth Brazil, a hundredth Brazil await the visitor.

37. Brazil does not represent a crisis in her marriage. There is no crisis in her marriage. She has no intention of leaving her husband; and her husband would be a fool if he left her. She is not in love with the Pole. At most she is sorry for him: sorry for his being lonely and old and out of touch with a world that is less and less receptive to his at-a-distance renderings of Chopin. Sorry for him too for his fixation on her (he may call it love but she does not).

38. Brazil in his company would be impossible. How would they spend their time when he is not playing Chopin to Brazilian high society? Taking walks on long white beaches amid bronzed Brazilian bodies? Dancing to Brazilian bands?

She likes familiar things. She likes being comfortable. She dislikes novelty for the sake of novelty. No wonder her husband finds her incurious.

Martynov, for example. She has never heard of Martynov, therefore she is ready to dislike his music. It does not reflect well on her.

39. Why is she castigating herself, making herself look foolish and complacent and even philistine? What has got into her?

40. She does not dream. She never dreams. She sleeps long and deeply and dreamlessly, and wakes in the morning refreshed, renewed. With her restful sleep and healthy way of life she will probably live to be a hundred.

Instead of dreaming she indulges her imagination. She can imagine all too well what a week in Brazil in the company of the Pole would be like. In particular she can imagine what it would be like if they slept together. She would have to pretend to be in ecstasies and he would have to pretend to believe her.

I absolve you: that is what she needs to say to him before they set foot on Brazilian soil. *I absolve you from all erotic duties. You sleep in your bed and I will sleep in mine.*

41. She wonders if he keeps a diary. *Diary of a Seducer.* Would he dare to put her in his diary? The week he spent in Brazil with a certain lady from Barcelona, 'who out of respect for her family shall remain nameless'.

THREE

1. An email arrives with an audio file attached: Chopin's B minor sonata. 'I record this for you alone. In English I cannot say what is in my heart, therefore I say it in music. Please listen, I pray to you.'

She obeys. She listens, paying hawk-like attention to the phrasing, the inflections, the minutest accelerations and decelerations—anything that could be construed as a private message. She comes up blank, baffled. It sounds just like his Deutsche Grammophon recording in the Concert Circle library. If he has smuggled in a message, it is in a code she does not know how to read.

2. Time passes. Another email: 'I will be in Mallorca in October for the Chopin festival. After Mallorca, perhaps your concert circle will invite me again. That is my warm hope.'

She writes back: 'Dear Witold, Thank you for the recording, and how good to hear you will be playing at the Chopin festival. Alas, the program of our Concert Circle is settled for the rest of the year. Yours, Beatriz.'

A day later she writes again. 'Dear Witold, It so happens that my husband's family owns a house near the town of Sóller, not far from Valldemossa, where the Chopin festival will be held. My husband and I will be spending some time there in October. Would you like to join us after your commitments? The house is spacious. You will have your own quarters. Let me know what you think. Yours, Beatriz.'

He writes back: 'Thank you, thank you, but I cannot be a friend of the family. Witold.' He adds a PS: '*A Friend of the Family* is a famous Polish novel. People call it the Polish *Werther*.'

She has heard of *Werther* but not of *A Friend of the Family*. Is there another coded message here? Does he expect her to track down *A Friend of the Family* and read it? Absurd man!

3. She speaks to her husband. 'Are we still going to Sóller in October?'

'Yes, if you like, if the house is free.'

'The house will be free. I thought of asking Tomás and Eva and the child.'

'Good! Good! Will you make the arrangements? But not for longer than a week.'

'I will make the arrangements, but I will probably stay on after you leave. A week is too short.'

She is not often duplicitous. She prefers frankness. She prefers laying her cards on the table. But sometimes laying one's cards on the table is not a good idea.

4. She speaks to Tomás, her son. 'Not possible,' he says. 'I can't take time off from work, and anyway it's no fun travelling with a baby.'

5. She books flights and calls the housekeeper in Sóller to instruct her to open up the house.

She enjoys making plans, settling details. If the Concert Circle runs smoothly, it is due to her diligence and her care for detail.

6. She has no intention of going to Valldemossa to hear the Pole play. Let him come to her.

Plotting. Plotting.

7. The house outside Sóller was bought during the 1940s by her husband's grandfather, who had made his fortune in shipping. At the time when he bought it, it was still the hub of a working farm, but over the years he sold off the farmland parcel by parcel, until he was left with only the big house and its outbuildings.

It was there that her husband spent his holidays as a child, and he still has a deep attachment to the place. He is deeply attached yet he visits less and less, she cannot understand why. She herself has come to love the old house, with its austere stonework and its high ceilings and its dim passages and the cool courtyard with its riot of plumbago and bougainvillea and the great old fig tree at its centre.

8. There is the question of conscience. Is her conscience going to plague her over her invitation to the Pole? Her conscience did not plague her over the young

man at the gymnasium whom she allowed to flirt with her last year and who once cornered her and tried to kiss her (she yielded her neck, her throat, but not her lips). Is it a question of territory? Is the gymnasium neutral ground whereas the house in Sóller is her husband's territory and the territory of his family going back two generations?

The Pole is in his seventies, in the evening of his years. The man at the gymnasium was in his twenties, with a vigorous male life stretching before him. The cases are hardly comparable. It would be forgivable if her husband were jealous of the man at the gymnasium but not if he were jealous of the Pole. A man of the Pole's age should not give rise to jealousy, he does not have that power. In any event, she has no intention of sleeping with him. When he comes to Sóller he can share her domestic routines. He can accompany her to the supermarket and help carry the groceries. He can dredge leaves out of the swimming pool. There is a piano in one of the spare rooms, an old upright: he can fix it up and play for her. By the end of the week his romantic fantasies will have gone up in smoke. He will have seen her as she truly is. He can then return to his native land a sadder and a wiser man.

9. 'Do you remember the Polish pianist who asked me to fly with him to Brazil?' she says to her husband. 'He is going to be in Mallorca at the same time as we are. He will be performing at the Chopin festival. Do you mind if I invite him to lunch?'

'Of course not. But wouldn't you rather see him by yourself?'

'No, I think he should see me *en famille*. That should bring him down to earth. He has rather elevated notions about me.'

Plotting.

10. Her invitation to the Pole is couched in unusually specific terms. If he wishes to see her, he should plan to arrive on such-and-such a date and depart on such-and-such a date. He should catch the number 203 bus from Valldemossa to the bus station in Sóller. If he calls in advance and informs her of his time of arrival, she will pick him up. He will be housed not in the main residence but in a cottage on the grounds. The cottage has a fully equipped kitchen, in case he wishes to cook for himself. Otherwise he is welcome to share meals with

her, Beatriz, his hostess, meals which will be prepared by the housekeeper. His time will be his own.

It reads, and is meant to read, like an invitation to a paying guest.

11. When the time comes, she and her husband travel to Sóller and enjoy a quiet week together. The weather is a little cool, a little windy, but nothing to complain about. The roads are empty, most of the tourists are gone. They drive to Banyalbufar, to Peguera, where she has a long, invigorating swim. They dine at a restaurant in Fornalutx that they have always been fond of.

12. 'What has happened about the Polish musician?' asks her husband. 'I thought he was coming to lunch.'

'The dates didn't work out,' she replies. 'He isn't free until next week, and you will be gone by then.'

'What a pity,' says her husband. 'I would have liked to meet him.'

He smiles. She smiles. They have navigated tricky passages before, they will navigate this one.

13. Her husband leaves. The Pole arrives. She picks him up at the bus station in the little Suzuki that they keep in Sóller. Nearly a year has passed since Girona. He has noticeably aged. He is in fact an old man.

Of course it is natural that he should have aged. Why should he be proof against the ravages of time? Nevertheless she is disappointed—more than disappointed, dismayed.

She wonders what the audiences in Valldemossa thought of him. *A spectre from the past*—is that what they thought? But perhaps, for some, he assumes an aura of timeless authority when he sits down at the keyboard.

14. He kisses her on both cheeks. 'So fresh you look, so beautiful,' he murmurs. His lips are dry, his skin soft, babyish: the skin of an old man.

15. They drive to the house in silence. The road up the hill is pitted, but she is a good driver, better than most of the men she knows. When they are on the island her husband leaves the driving to her. 'I know I am in safe hands,' he says.

16. She shows the Pole to his cottage. 'I will leave you to unpack and settle in. When lunch is ready Loreto will ring the bell.'

'You are gracious,' says the Pole.

Gracious: what an old-fashioned, bookish word. Does it have a meaning any longer? *Ave Maria, gratia plena, ora pro nobis.*

17. He responds promptly to the lunchtime bell. He has changed his clothes. He now wears sandals, cream-coloured slacks, a sky-blue shirt. He bears a Panama hat, ready for what the afternoon will bring.

She introduces him to Loreto. *No habla español,* she tells Loreto. He doesn't speak Spanish. Loreto gives him a tight smile, a nod. *Señor.*

Loreto looks after this house and another, further down the valley, belonging to a Mexican. She arrives and leaves on a 125 cc moped. Her husband is an odd-job man and gardener. They have a son and a daughter, both grown up, both married, both living on the mainland.

Nothing about Loreto is surprising. That is to say, of what she knows about Loreto nothing surprises her, not even the moped. But of course Loreto has a life of her own, invisible to her employers, which may well be full of surprises. It may contain, for instance, Loreto's equivalent of the Pole: a man who finds her, Loreto, to be full of grace and worth pursuing. It is only a matter of chance that the story being told is not about Loreto and her man but about her, Beatriz, and her Polish admirer. Another fall of the dice and the story would be about Loreto's submerged life.

18. 'I hope you are hungry. Loreto has made us old-style *tumbet*. Do you know it? Did they serve it in Vall-demossa? In Catalonia we have a similar dish but we call it *samfaina*.'

She has always been a good hostess, skilled at putting guests at their ease. It is particularly important to put the Pole at his ease, to make him feel at home, so that when he leaves it will be with pleasant memories.

'Your husband did not come?' says the Pole.

'My husband came, but then was called back to his office. He sends his regrets. He is sorry he could not meet you.'

'He is a good man, your husband?'

What a strange question. 'Yes, I believe he is a good man. It is not hard to be good, in our times.'

'Yes? You think so?'

'I do. We live in fortunate times. In fortunate times it is not hard to be good. Do you think otherwise?'

'I do not live in fortunate times. But I try to be good.'

She does not see how the person sitting on one side of the table can live in fortunate times while the person on the other side of the table does not, but she lets it pass. 'Tell me about your daughter the singer. She lives in Germany, I remember you saying. How is she getting on?'

'I will show you.' He takes out his phone and shows her a picture of a tall, serious-looking girl in her teens dressed all in white. 'It is an old picture, from the old days, but I keep it. Now it is different. She is married, she lives in Berlin, she and her husband have a restaurant, a grand success, which brings them much money. The singing? That is in the past, I think. So: successful, yes, but not happy. Not blessed.'

Not blessed. It is sometimes hard to know what the man means, with his incomplete English. Is he saying something profound or is he simply hitting the wrong words, like a monkey sitting in front of a typewriter?

Are people with much money truly not happy? She has much money and is happy, more or less. The Pole must have much money too, after all his concerts, and does not seem unhappy. Gloomy perhaps, but not miserable. Perhaps he means that the daughter in Berlin is discontented. Discontent is not uncommon. Discontent: not knowing what one wants.

'Do you see her often? Do you and she get along together?'

The Pole raises his hands, palms upwards, in a gesture she cannot decode. Where she comes from it means *Have courage, press on!* but where he comes from it could mean something quite different—*There is nothing to be done*, for example.

'We are civilized,' says the Pole. 'But she does not have my soul. She has her mother's soul.'

Civilized. How to translate? *We do not fly at each other's throat? We do not yawn in each other's face? We greet each other with a kiss on the cheek?* Whatever the case, being civilized in each other's company does not seem much of an achievement for a father and daughter.

'Fortunately,' she says, 'my children and I share the same soul. The same dispositions. We have the same blood running in our veins.'

'That is good,' says the Pole.

'Yes, it is good. I invited my elder son to join us here in Sóller. He is a serious person. You would like him. Unfortunately, he could not come. He and his wife have a new baby, and his wife finds it a strain to travel. One can understand.'

'So you are a grandmother now.'

'Yes. I will be fifty on my next birthday. Were you aware of that?'

'A gentleman does not ask a lady's age.'

He delivers this pronouncement with a straight face. Does he never smile? Does he have no sense of the ridiculous?

'It sometimes happens,' she says, 'that what a gentleman does not ask of a lady turns out to be what the gentleman in question does not want to know about the lady. What the gentleman would find unpleasing to know. Because it would upset some of the ideas about the lady that the gentleman holds. Some of his preconceptions.'

The Pole breaks off a wedge of bread, dips it in the sauce, makes no reply. Loreto, in the far corner of the kitchen, pretends to be washing the pans, but her manner suggests that she is listening. Perhaps she knows more English than she lets on.

'Have you finished?' she says. 'Have you had enough? Would you like coffee?'

19. Loreto serves them coffee in the living room, where the huge windows (an innovation of her husband's) allow a view over the valley and its almond groves.

'So, Witold, here you are at last, in sunny Mallorca in the company of your elusive lady friend. Are you happy at last?'

'Dearest lady, I do not have the words. Not the words in English, not the words in any language. But gratitude, yes. Gratitude comes up from my heart, you can see it.' With two hands he makes a strange, awkward gesture, as if opening his ribcage from the bottom and lifting out the contents.

'I see it, I believe it. But your grand design still escapes me—your design, your plan. Why are you here, now that you are here? What do you want from your friend?'

'Dear lady, perhaps we can be like normal people and do normal things—no? Without a plan. A normal man and a normal woman do not have a plan.'

'Really? Do you think so? That is not my experience.

In my experience normal men and normal women very often have plans relative to each other. Designs. But let us pretend we have no plan. Then let me ask: when you go back to Poland, and your friends say to you, "So you spent a week on the island of Mallorca with a lady friend! What was it like?" how will you reply? Will you say that it was okay, nothing out of the normal about it? That it was just like being in Poland except that the sun was shining?'

The Pole gives a laugh, a short, explosive burst. It is the first time she has heard him laugh. 'Always you push me in a corner,' he says. 'You know I am not clever like you in the English language. If not *normal*, what is a better word in English?'

'*Normal* is a good word. Nothing wrong with it.'

'*Ordinary*,' he says. 'Maybe *ordinary* is better. I wish to live with you. That is the wish of my heart. I wish to live with you until I die. In an ordinary way. Side by side. So.' He clasps his hands tightly together. 'An ordinary life side by side—that is what I want. For always. The next life too, if there is another life. But if not, okay, I accept. If you say no, not for the rest of life, just for this week—okay, I accept that too. For just a day even. For just a minute. A minute is enough. What is time? Time

71

is nothing. We have our memory. In memory there is no time. I will hold you in my memory. And you, maybe you will remember me too.'

'Of course I will remember you, you strange man.'

She utters the words without forethought, hears them echo startlingly in her mind's ear. What is she saying? How can she promise to remember him when she has every reason to believe that the episode of the Polish musician who paid her a visit in Sóller is going to fade and fade until on her deathbed it is less than a speck of dust?

The man seems to trust in the powers of memory. She would like to tell him about the powers of forgetting. How much has she not forgotten! And she is a normal person, an ordinary person, not an exception at all.

What has she forgotten? She has no idea. It is gone, has vanished from the face of the earth as if it had never existed.

20. She rouses herself. 'Shall we go for a walk?' she says. 'Have you brought walking shoes? The wind picks up in the late afternoon, so if we want to go it is best we go now.'

The Pole changes his shoes and they go for their walk, following a track that will take them to the crest of the hill overlooking the town. He is slow but not as slow as she feared he might be.

'What is Poland like?' she says. 'I have never been there, as you know.'

'Poland is not beautiful like this. Poland is full of rubbish. Centuries of rubbish. We do not bury it. We do not hide it. To love Poland you must be born there. You will not love my country, if you come.'

'But you love Poland.'

'I love Poland and I hate Poland. This is not special. For many Poles it is true.'

'Your master—Frédéric Chopin—left Poland and never went back. You could have done the same.'

'Yes, I could say goodbye to Poland and buy an apartment in Valldemossa and wait for some French lady to arrive, some George Sand who is tired of French men with crude habits, who wants a gentle Pole to give her love to. Or I could find an apartment in Barcelona. But that would not be good for you, so I don't do it. It is the truth—no?'

Indeed, indeed! Indeed it is the truth! It would indeed not be good for her to have this man hovering at her doorstep, casting his shadow over her. 'I agree. It would be a very bad idea for you to be living in Barcelona. Bad for me and perhaps even worse for you.'

But why is he bringing up George Sand? Whatever he has in mind, she finds the thought distasteful: herself as his foreign mistress, his part-time nurse.

They have reached the crest. There they halt, gazing out over the coastline. Lovers would put their arms around each other. Lovers might even kiss. But not they.

'About this evening,' she says: 'would you like to go out or shall I cook for us? There are one or two good restaurants in Sóller. Or we could drive further afield.'

'The lady—Loreta is her name?—she does not cook for you?'

'Loreto does not come in every day. Also, her working day ends at three. If we want her to come back in the evening I will have to make a special arrangement.'

'Tonight I prefer we stay at home. Tomorrow I take you to a restaurant. But tonight we stay at home and I help you cook.'

'Very well, we stay at home. I cook, but you do not help.' She has a vision of the Pole in the kitchen, blundering around, knocking things over, getting in the way. 'I cook and you take a rest.' It is like talking to a child.

21. For supper she makes a big omelette with herbs from the garden, and a salad. She is determined that everything remain simple. If the man is still hungry there is always bread.

They have a good cellar here in Sóller. Stocking the cellar is her husband's department. She does not drink much; the Pole drinks more.

'I have a gift for you,' says the Pole.

She unties the ribbon, lifts the lid of the little box. Inside is what appears to be a pine cone.

'It is a rose,' he explains.

It is indeed a rose, carved with considerable delicacy in a blond wood.

'It's very pretty,' she says.

'It is from the house of the Chopins, the parents of Frédéric. It is folk art in Poland. Mainly this folk art is for religion, for the altar in the church. But the parents of Frédéric were not religious, so this was in the house for décor, with other flowers. In their time it was painted, but the paint is gone, it is two hundred years in the past, and to me it is more beautiful with just the wood. I don't know how you call the wood in English. In Polish it is *świerk*.'

So she is to become custodian of a relic of the sainted

Chopin. Is she the right person for the job, who does not believe in God, much less in Chopin? 'Thank you, Witold,' she says. 'It is beautiful. I will treasure it. But I am going to say goodnight now. I go to bed early. It is not a very Spanish habit, but for me it is so. You will have to retire too, I am afraid. I have to lock the house, I cannot sleep easily if the house is not locked. I will leave a light on outside. Goodnight.' She presents her cheek to be kissed. 'Sleep well.'

22. Usually she falls asleep at once. But not tonight. Has she made a mistake, inviting the Pole to Sóller? *I want to live side by side with you like two clasped hands. In the next life too.* What sentimental nonsense! *You give me peace.* And a rose from the home of his hero. *For you!* What a joke!

The rest of the week yawns before her. How are they going to occupy their time? With rambles? With idiot conversations? With visits to the beach, visits to restaurants? How much of such a routine can they bear—two polite, civilized, normal people—before one of them snaps? And this was supposed to be a vacation!

What does the man want? What does *she* want?

23. It is daytime. They have had breakfast.

'I have something to show you,' she says. She conducts him to one of the back rooms, where a piano has stood, covered with a dust sheet, for as long as she can remember.

She removes the sheet. 'Have a look at it,' she says. 'Is it any good?'

He shrugs. 'It is old,' he says. 'It is made in Spain. Spain is not famous for pianos.' He plays a scale. The keys are slow and sticky, a hammer is missing, the strings are badly out of tune. 'You have tools?'

'Piano tools? No.'

'Not piano tools, just tools like you use for a machine.'

She shows him the toolbox in the garage. He selects a spanner and a pair of pliers and spends an hour working on the piano. Then he sits down and plays a simple piece, made quaint by the click of the missing hammer.

'I am sorry we don't have anything better to offer you,' she says.

'You remember Orfeo? Orfeo did not have a piano, just a harp, very primitive, but the animals came and listened to him, the lion, the tiger, the horse, the cow, all of them. Congress of peace.'

Orfeo. So now he is Orfeo.

24. They drive down to the port and have coffee on a terrace above the harbour. She asks him about his time in Valldemossa. 'Did you find the audiences there receptive? I mean, did they appreciate your playing?'

'I played in the old monastery. The acoustics are not good. But the audience—yes, in the audience there were serious people, some of them.'

'Is that what you like—serious people? Do I count as a serious person?'

He looks her up and down. 'In Polish we talk of a person who is heavy, a person who is not made of air. You are a heavy person.'

She laughs. 'In English they say *solid—a solid person* or *a person of substance. Heavy* is reserved for fat people. I am glad to hear you don't think I am made of air, but you are wrong, I am not solid, not a person of substance.'

She thinks: *If you now say I am liquid, then I will begin to believe in you.* But he does not.

I am liquid. If you tried to hold me, I would flow out of your hands like water.

'You, on the other hand,' she says, 'are solid. Perhaps too solid for Chopin. Has anyone ever told you that?'

'Many people think Chopin is made of air,' he says. 'I try to correct them.'

'There is plenty of air in Chopin. And even more water. Running water. Liquid music. Debussy too.'

He inclines his head. Yes? No? She does not know how to interpret his gestures. Perhaps she never will. A foreigner.

'That is how I see it,' she says. 'But what do I know? In music I am just an amateur.'

25. He spends the afternoon in the back room improvising at the piano. Since she hears no clicking noises, she presumes that he is managing to skirt the dead key. Not lacking in ingenuity.

While he is occupied she ventures into the cottage that is now his territory. The bathroom bears a faint smell of eau de Cologne. Abstractedly she examines his travelling kit, neatly laid out on the shelf beneath the mirror. A razor. A hairbrush with an ebony handle. Pomade. Shampoo. An array of pillboxes, each with a label in Polish. A man from another era. Or perhaps all of Poland is like this: stuck in the past. Why is she so incurious about Poland?

26. She asks him to play for her. 'Play those little pieces by Lutosławski that you played in Barcelona.'

He plays the first three, with a click for the missing F.

'That is enough?'

'Yes, that is enough. I just wanted a change from Chopin.'

27. 'After Mallorca, where do you go?' she asks him.

'I have engagements in Russia. One in Saint Petersburg, one in Moscow.'

'Are you famous in Russia? Excuse my ignorance. I mean, do the Russians regard you highly?'

'No one regards me highly, nowhere in the world. It's okay. I am the old generation. I am history. I should be in a museum, in a glass cabinet. But here I am. I am still alive. *It is a miracle*, I say to them. *If you don't believe, you can touch me.*'

She is confused. Who does not believe? Who is being invited to touch him? The Russians?

'You ought to be proud of yourself,' she says. 'Not everyone enters history. There are people who spend their whole lives trying to be part of history and fail. I will never be part of history, for example.'

'But you do not try,' he says.

'No, I don't try. I am content to be who I am.'

What she does not say is: *Why should I want to end up in history? What is history to me?*

28. 'Is there a coiffeur in this town?' he asks.

'Several. What do you need done? If all you need is a haircut, I can do it for you. I cut my sons' hair for years. I am perfectly competent.'

It is, to a degree, a test. How vain is he about that leonine head of hair?

Not vain at all, as it turns out. 'For you to cut my hair—it would be the greatest gift,' he says.

She seats him on the porch with a sheet around his neck. He declines a mirror: his faith in her seems absolute. Through the operation he sits without opening his eyes, a dreamy smile on his lips. Is the touch of her fingers on his scalp all that it takes to satisfy him? Caressing someone's head: an unexpectedly intimate act.

'Your hair is very fine,' she says. 'More like a woman's than a man's.' What she does not say is that he is beginning to grow bald at the crown. But perhaps he knows.

Her father had a nurse to look after him in his last

weeks and months. However, it was often she, Beatriz, who was called in to help. It was not a role she had been prepared for, yet she performed it quite adequately, to her own surprise. If the Pole were to fall ill now, she would look after him. She would find that perfectly natural. What is unnatural is that he arrives at her door not as an old man in need of care but as a would-be lover.

29. 'You have never told me about your marriage,' she says. 'Was it a happy marriage?'

'My marriage is long ago in the past. And in communist Poland too. Nineteen seventy-eight it was over. Nineteen seventy-eight is almost history.'

'Just because your marriage is history does not mean it was not real. Memories are real—you said so yourself. You must have memories.'

The Pole gives one of his little inward smiles. 'Some of us remember good memories. Some of us remember bad memories. We choose which memories we remember. Some memories, we put them in the underground. That is how you say it: the underground?'

'Yes, that is how they say it. The underground. The cemetery of bad memories. Tell me some of your good memories. What was your wife like? What was her name?'

'Her name was Małgorzata but everyone called her Gosia. She was a teacher. She taught English and German languages. From her I perfected my English.'

'Do you have a photograph of her?'

'No.'

Of course not. Why would he?

He does not ask about her own marriage and its associated memories, good and bad. He does not ask whether she carries a photograph of her husband wherever she goes. He does not ask about anything. Truly incurious.

30. That is one of the more intimate conversations they have. For the rest, when they are together, they are silent. She is not normally silent—with friends she can be exuberant, chatty—but from the Pole there seems to emanate a freeze on all frivolity. She tells herself it is a matter of the language—that if she were Polish or he were Spanish they would talk more easily, like any normal couple. But if he were Spanish he would be a different man, just as if she were Polish she would be

a different woman. They are what they are: grown-ups, civilized people.

31. She takes him out to lunch in Fornalutx—not to the intimate little restaurant that she and her husband frequent but to one attached to a hotel that a century ago was the residence of a local eminence. At its centre is a courtyard open to the skies: birds swoop in and strut around among the tables or dip themselves in the fountain. No one is curious about the two of them, no one shows any interest. They are free beings, answerable to none.

She visits the ladies' room. Emerging from the shadows, she pauses in the doorway, waiting for him to catch sight of her, then threads her way towards him through the tables. His eyes are fixed on her, as are the eyes of the two waiters.

She is aware of the effect she can have on men. Grace: not such an antique concept after all. In Poland or Russia, she thinks, he will relive this moment, the moment when, crossing the floor towards him, came a vision of grace embodied. *What have we done to deserve this,* he will think, *guests, cooks, waiters, all of us? Grace that descends from the skies, shedding its radiance on us.*

32. It is their third day together in the house. Loreto has done her chores and gone home. She, Beatriz, tries to read but is too distracted. Time moves sluggishly. She wills it to pass.

Dusk falls. She taps at the cottage door. 'Witold? I have made us something to eat.'

They eat in silence. Afterwards she says: 'I am going to clear up, then I am going to retire. I will leave the back door unlocked. If you feel lonely during the night and want to visit, do so.'

That is all she says. She does not want a discussion.

She brushes her teeth, washes her face, combs her hair, inspects herself in the bathroom mirror. Looking at oneself in a mirror is something that women do in books and films, but she is not in a book or a film and she is not looking at herself. No, it is the being on the other side of the glass who is looking at her, to whose inspection she is submitting herself. What does that other see?

With an intense effort she tries to send herself through the glass, to inhabit that alien self, that alien gaze. No use.

She puts on her black nightdress, parts the curtains, switches off the light. Moonlight pours in. She is still a good-looking woman: there is that to hold on to. *Amazing, the way you have kept your looks!* says Margarita. *Two children and you still have the figure of an eighteen-year-old!* Well, let him marvel at his luck. But what would the two children in question say if they could see her now? *Mama, how could you!*

She hears the back door open, hears his footsteps, hears him enter the bedroom. Without a word he undresses; she averts her eyes. She feels his body stretch out beside hers, feels the barrel chest against her and the hair that covers it in a thick mat. *Like a bear!* she thinks. *What am I letting myself in for? Too late: no going back now.*

She helps him as best she can with the lovemaking. Though she has no experience of old men, she can guess what their troubles in bed will be, their deficiencies. It is a strange experience, and not a little frightening, to have that huge weight pressing down on her, but before long it is over.

'So now you have had me,' she says. 'You have had your gracious lady. Are you at last content?'

'My heart is full,' he says. He presses her hand to his chest. Dimly she can feel the beating of a heart, *trip-trip-trip*, faster than her own steady heart—in fact alarmingly fast. The last thing she wants is a corpse in her bed.

'I don't know what a full heart feels like,' she says, 'as opposed to an empty heart. But you must be careful. Do you hear me? Do you understand?'

'I hear you, *cariño*.'

Cariño. Where on earth did he pick that up?

33. She is not going to spend the night with this huge lump of a man in her bed. 'I must sleep now,' she says, 'and you must go. I will see you in the morning. Good-night, Witold. Sleep well.'

She watches his shadowy outline as he puts on his clothes. A gleam of light as he opens the door, then he is gone.

Three more nights in Sóller. Is he going to expect her to accommodate him on each of them? A wave of tiredness sweeps over her. She wishes she were back in

Barcelona in her own bed, in her own life, without these complications. She wishes, above all, to sleep.

34. She takes particular care, in the morning, with her clothes, with her makeup. By the time she appears in the kitchen the Pole has finished his breakfast. She offers her cheek to be kissed.

'Did you sleep well?' she asks. He nods.

Over her bowl of fruit she inspects him. How does he seem? Confused, mainly. Probably sleepless too.

You have only yourself to blame, she chides herself. Two strangers thrown together in the dark, performing an act neither was ready for. Actors. Performers. *You thought you would get away scot-free, you thought there would be no consequences, but you were wrong, wrong, wrong.*

'How about we go for a swim?' she offers. 'Have you brought a swimsuit? No? We can buy you one in Sóller if you like.'

They visit an outfitter's. Yellow is the only colour they have in the Pole's size.

It is still early. At her favourite beach the family groups have not yet arrived. The only people there are the serious swimmers.

It is a strange experience for the two of them, who mere hours ago were naked in bed together, to behold each other semi-naked in the glare of sunlight. What does she see? How thin, even spindly, his legs are. She hopes he will not notice the tracery of blue veins on her inner thighs.

You give me peace. Body wrestling against sweaty body. As much of a shock for the man as for the woman. After a duel like that, no room left for adoration, for veneration. Adoration sent packing.

In the water they part company. He stays in the shallows, she heads straight out into the deep.

Alone in the sea: a profound relief. She could dive down, metamorphose into a dolphin, feel the whole mess she has created wash away. What a stupid idea to invite a strange man to her husband's childhood home!

35. They are back at the house. 'I want to speak to you about Loreto,' she says. 'Loreto is a woman, she has a woman's eye. There is no point in trying to conceal from her what is going on. Nevertheless, we cannot be flagrant. Do you understand what I am saying? We can-

not insult her by carrying on an adultery—because that is what it is, that is its name—under her nose. She has her pride. She will walk out and not come back. And I will be humiliated.'

'I understand,' says the Pole. 'We do not behave like lovers.'

'Correct. We do not behave like lovers.'

'I have been your lover since the day I met you and no one knows. No one in the world can guard a secret better than I can.'

'If you really believe that then you are a fool. To me you are transparent. To Loreto you are transparent. To any woman you are transparent. What I am asking you to do has nothing to do with guarding secrets. I am asking you to maintain a fiction. Can you do that, in a respectful way?'

The Pole bows his head. 'Dante the poet was the lover of Beatrice and no one knew.'

'That is nonsense. Beatrice knew. All her friends knew. They giggled about it, like all girls do. Do you really think you are Dante, Witold?'

'No, I am not Dante. I am not inspired. And I am not clever with words.'

36. In the afternoon they go for a walk, following the same route up the hillside.

'Tell me more about your daughter,' she says. 'Does she take after you or after her mother?'

'If she looks like me it would be a disaster. No, she looks like her mother.'

'And her inner life? Does she follow her mother in her passions or does she follow you?'

'Yes? No? I cannot say. A daughter does not show to her father her passions.'

She lets it pass. *Passion*: what does he think the word means? Naked bodies on a summer night?

All their conversations seem to be like that: coins passed back and forth in the dark, in ignorance of what they are worth.

Sometimes she has the feeling that he is not listening to what she says, only to the tone of her voice, as if she were singing rather than speaking. She is not fond of her own voice—too low, too soft—but he seems to drink it in. Always he sees the best in her.

Something unnatural in loving without expecting to be loved in return.

Why is she with him? Why has she brought him here?

J. M. Coetzee

What if anything does she find pleasing about him? There is an answer: that he so transparently takes pleasure in her. When she walks into the room, his face, usually so dour, lights up. In the gaze that bathes her there is a quantum of male desire, but finally it is a gaze of admiration, of dazzlement, as though he cannot believe his luck. It pleases her to offer herself to his gaze.

She has come to like his hands too. It amuses her to think that he makes his living by manual labour.

There are other features, however, that irritate her: his stiffness, his remoteness from the world around him, above all the pompous way he talks. Everything he says, everything he does has a formal feel to it. Even in her arms he does not seem able to relax. A comical spectacle, the two of them, making their love in English, a tongue whose erotic reaches are closed to them.

Is she too hard on him? Does she lack tenderness? Is each of us born with a certain quota of tenderness, and did she expend all her tenderness on her husband and children, leaving nothing for this late lover?

If she does not love him, what is the name of the feeling she has for him, the feeling that has led her down this questionable path?

If she had to pin it down, she would call it pity. He fell

in love with her and she took pity on him and out of pity gave him his desire. That was how it happened; that was her mistake.

37. Her husband telephones. 'How are you getting on with your musician friend?' he asks.

'Not too badly. He came in yesterday by bus from Vall-demossa. He has fixed up the piano in the back room, as far as it can be fixed, which will be useful for us. I'll take him for a drive this afternoon and show him some of the island. He leaves tomorrow.'

'And at a personal level?'

'At a personal level? He and I get along perfectly well. He is a bit *arisco*, a bit dour, but I don't mind that.'

She is unused to lying, but on the telephone it is not so difficult. And they do not count as great lies. In the end they will amount to nothing. Whatever occurred here in Sóller will be swept into the past and forgotten.

38. On each of the three nights left to them the Pole visits her in her bed. She is reminded of the story of the Greek girl who, nervous that the dark stranger in her

bed might turn out to be a monster, lit a lamp and discovered he was a god. Well, she, Beatriz, needs no lamp. The stranger in her bed may not be a monster but he is certainly no god.

Why did the girl need to see her visitor anyway? Was the weight, the crushing pressure of an alien male body, not enough?

The shock of the new. A bright shock, like being electrocuted, not a dark one, like being swept away and buried in a mudslide.

There is a moment on the second night when out of the past there re-emerges the delicious feeling of falling. She had thought it gone forever, that it belonged only to youth or even to childhood: the terror and delight of shooting down a water slide, when the will is abdicated and one is, briefly, pure experience.

What else does she remember? Fingers playing on her skin, drawing music out of her. A musician's touch.

Sometimes, while he is about his erotic business, her mind drifts idly to the shopping she must ask Loreto to do, to the appointment she has missed with the dentist.

As a lover the man is capable but not quite capable enough. No matter how resolute the spirit, he cannot prevent the creakiness of his physical being, his lack of vital force, from infecting his lovemaking. He covers up for it as best he can, and, each time he takes his departure from her bed, thanks her: 'I thank you from my heart.' Her own heart goes out to him at those moments, in pity if not in love. So hard to be a man!

She cannot bring herself to caress him. He is aware, she knows, of this reluctance on her part, this physical distaste. Awareness of it enters into his ritual thanks. *Thank you for descending so far.*

She ought to feel guilty. One should not go to bed with a man whom one does not desire. But she feels no guilt. *I give enough,* she says to herself. *And it is not forever.*

39. *Be-a-triz,* he whispers into her ear. *I will die with your name on my lips.*

40. She is in his arms. It is their last night together. She speaks. 'This is not easy to say, Witold, but tonight we have come to the end. We are not going to see each other again. It makes life too difficult for me. I do not need to explain. Just accept it.'

She is glad they are in the dark. She does not like

hurting people; she does not want to see a stricken look of any kind on his face.

'Don't think badly of me. Please. There is a bus to Valldemossa at eight-fifteen. I will drive you to the bus station.'

She has rehearsed her speech beforehand, therefore it is understandable that the moment should feel artificial, as though she were standing somewhere outside, or hovering overhead, hearing the woman's voice, watching for the man's reaction.

The man reacts by slackening his embrace, which a moment ago was warm but has now turned cold; he reacts by turning away from her, getting up, reaching for his clothes. He reacts by finding his way to the door (with a slight stumble in the dark) and making his exit; if she listens hard she can hear the click as the kitchen door closes behind him.

She allows herself to exhale. She is glad, unutterably glad, that he did not react with anger, with hurt pride, that he did not humiliate himself by pleading. If he had pleaded she would have turned against him forever.

41. He does make a plea, after all, one last plea, on the way to the bus the next morning. 'After Russia is fin-

ished we can fly to Brazil,' he says. 'You can swim in the sea in Brazil.'

'No,' she says. 'I am not going to follow you around the world—you or any other man. No.'

They arrive at the bus stop. 'I am not going to wait,' she says. 'Goodbye.' She kisses him on the lips. Then she is gone.

42. Back home she checks the cottage. He has left no trace behind, no physical trace. A good guest.

43. *'El señor vuelve?'* asks Loreto.

'No, el señor ha sido llamado de vuelta a su tierra natal. A Polonia. No volverá.' The gentleman will not be coming back.

44. For the rest of the day she goes about her routines slowly, calmly, deliberately. She is still in a state of shock, she recognizes, and has been so ever since the Pole first manifested himself in her bedroom. If she can stay calm and allow time to do its work, the state of

shock—which she pictures as a sheet wound around her so tightly that she can barely breathe—will lose its grip and life will resume its accustomed orderliness.

A sheet or else a frame, like the one in the Greek story, a bed in which one's limbs are crushed until one fits someone else's idea of how one should be.

The Pole too, for all she knows. The Pole, with his inconveniently long legs and big hands, may have been crushed and contorted in a frame of his own.

45. In the days before she flies back to Barcelona she has time to reorder her memories and settle on the story she is going to tell herself, the story that will become her story. She *had a fling*, she decides (she uses the English term). She had a fling with a visiting musician, which had its rewards but is now over. If Margarita, who is intuitive, taxes her with it (*You have been with someone! I can see it!*), she will not dissemble. *It was that Polish pianist you brought to Barcelona—you remember him? He was playing at the Chopin festival. He was free, I was free, we spent a few days together. Nothing serious. I am sure he has lots of affairs.*

She is prepared to entertain the possibility that her story may be incomplete and even in certain respects untrue. But, looking into her heart, she can find no dark residue: no regret, no sorrow, no longings—nothing to trouble the future.

Nothing serious. Is love a state of mind, a state of being, a phenomenon, a fashion that recedes, even as we watch it, into the past, into the backward reaches of history? The Pole was in love with her, *seriously* in love— and probably still is—but the Pole himself is a relic of history, of an age when desire had to be infused with a tincture of the unattainable before it could pass as the real thing. What of her, Beatriz, his beloved? Well, she was certainly not unattainable. On the contrary, she was all too attainable. *Come and visit me in my house. Come and visit me in my bed.* If she has saved herself, in the end, from the stigma of the too easily attainable, it was only by sending the Pole packing—the Pole who is no doubt at this very moment working up a story of his own about a cruel Spanish mistress who left a scar on his heart that will take a long time to heal.

FOUR

1. For a while after her return to Barcelona she continues in a state of mild shock. It surprises her that what occurred in Mallorca can have an effect so long-lasting, like a bomb that explodes harmlessly but leaves one deafened.

Being in a state of shock does not prevent her from plunging back into activity. She has been drafted onto a committee to fund residencies for rising young musicians: she spends hours every day on the telephone. And then there is the Concert Circle, whose audiences are dwindling as regulars grow old or infirm. Tomás Lesinski has died; his wife Ester is in the process of moving to France to live with their daughter. The grant that the Circle receives from the city is about to be slashed by half ('financial stringencies'): they will have to trim their programme from ten concerts a year to six.

She does not miss the Pole, not at all. He writes to her. She deletes his letters without reading them.

2. In October of 2019, visiting the Sala Mompou, she is told by a secretary that someone is trying to contact her from Germany. 'It is about a musician who once played here, I didn't catch the name, it sounded Russian. She left her number.'

She calls the number and hears a recorded message in German. Speaking English, she leaves her name.

Her call is returned. 'This is Ewa Reichert, my father is Witold Walczykiewicz, he passed away, perhaps you know this?'

'No, I did not know. I am sorry. Please accept my condolences.'

'He was ill for a long time.'

'I knew nothing of this. I am afraid I lost touch with your father some time ago. He will be remembered. He was a great pianist.'

'Yes. There are some things for you that he left behind.'

'Oh? What kind of things?'

'I have not seen. They are still in Warsaw, in the apartment. You were there?'

'I have never been to Warsaw, Mrs Reichert, Ewa. I have never been to Poland. Are you sure you have the right person?'

'This is the number that I called, and now you call me, so it is you—no?'

'I understand. Can you send these items to me?'

'I am in Berlin, I cannot send anything. I give you the name of the neighbour in Warsaw, then you can make arrangements. Her name is Pani Jablońska, for a long time she was a friend of my father. All the items for you she has put in a box with your name. Only you must act soon. I wait only for the documents from the lawyer, then I sell the apartment. Or perhaps it is not important to you, I don't know, it is your decision. But I say again, you must please act soon. There is a *wohltätige Organisation* in Warsaw, I don't know how you say it in English: I arrange that they come and take away everything in the apartment, make it clean, that is how they work. So if you want these things, you call Pani Jablońska.'

She dictates an address and telephone number in Warsaw.

'Thank you. I will speak to Pani Jablońska and see what can be done. You have no idea what these things are that your father wanted me to have?'

'No. My father did never tell me his secrets. Also, Pani Jablońska will not speak English, so you must have translation when you telephone.'

'Thank you. Thank you for letting me know. Goodbye.'

Secrets. So she is one of the Pole's secrets: the Barcelona secret. What other secrets did he leave behind in cities around the world?

3. She calls a courier company. Yes, they operate in Poland, they operate everywhere in Europe. Yes, they can pick up a consignment from an address in Warsaw. What does the consignment consist of? A box? A large box? A small box? For an item of under five kilograms, for door-to-door pick-up and delivery, the charge will be one hundred and eighty Euros, plus customs duties if there are customs duties, depending on what is in the box. What is in the box? Photographs? CDs? Used CDs?

Normally there no customs duties on such items within the EU. Shall they go ahead?

First let me make arrangements for the pick-up, she says. I will call you back.

4. One of the violinists in the chamber orchestra that uses the Sala Mompou is a Russian. She catches him after a rehearsal. 'Can you spare me a minute? I need to get a message to a lady in Poland. I have her number here. If I call her, can you speak to her and give her a message—that a courier will be coming on Friday to fetch the box? Can you do that for me?'

'I don't speak Polish,' says the violinist. 'Polish is not Russian, is different language.'

'Yes, I know, but this is an elderly lady, she has lived through a lot of history, she must know some Russian, and it is a very simple message.'

'Speak Russian to Poles is like insult, but for you I try. Courier is coming Friday?'

'Courier is coming Friday, she must give him the box.' She taps in Pani Jablońska's number and hands over the phone.

There is no reply.

'Write the text in Russian and I will send it. The text is: *Good day, Pani Jablońska. My name is Beatriz, I am the friend of Pan Witold. A courier will come on Friday. Please give the box to the courier.*'

'I write in Roman alphabet,' says the violinist. He writes: *Dobri den, Pani Jablońska. Menya zovut Beatriz, ya drug* . . . You write his name. *Kuryer priyedet v pyatnitsu. Pazhaluysta, otdayte korobku kuryeru.* 'Is not good Russian, but maybe Polish lady understands. I go now. You tell me if you have success, yes?' And he hurries off.

There is no reply to the Russian's text. Early the next morning, with the Russian words at hand ready to be repeated, she telephones Pani Jablońska. Again there is no reply. She calls at all hours, that day and that night, without result.

5. What can the Pole have left for her? Whatever it is, can it be worth all this fuss? Does she want to hear yet more of his recordings of Chopin?

The future lies open before her and the Pole is trying to draw her back. From the grave he stretches out a great claw to drag her into the past. Well, she does not have to submit. She can shrug off the claw. To the courier man she can say, *Cancel my order*. To the daughter she can say, *It is too much trouble, speaking Russian gibberish to Pani Jablońska, who will not understand anyway. So go ahead, clear out your father's apartment, sell everything, be rid of it*. To the man in the grave she can say, *You have no power over me. You are dead. Being dead may be a new experience for you but you will get used to it. It is a not uncommon fate to find oneself dead and forgotten*.

6. She telephones the daughter again, Ewa. 'I have been in touch with a courier company. They say they can fetch the box, no problem. The problem is Pani Jablońska. She does not answer my calls. Perhaps something has happened to her—I don't know. Is there anyone else who can give the box to the courier?'

'There is the *Agentur*, they are selling the apartment, they have keys. You can call the *Agentur* and explain, yes?'

'Explain what, Ewa?' She cannot keep the sharpness from her voice.

There are noises in the background. '*Ich komme!*' cries Ewa. 'I must go now. I send you the number of the *Agentur*, then you can explain. Goodbye.'

Explain what?

7. The apartment is not at all what she had expected. To begin with, it is not in Warsaw proper but in the outer suburbs. From the street where the taxi drops her she has to cross a car park and a playground where three boys are racing their bicycles, with a little white dog scurrying after them, yapping and trying to bite their tyres. And then the apartment block itself is devoid of all character, built to the same drab plan as blocks in the working-class sections of Barcelona. Why would he choose to live here of all places?

Early for her appointment, she makes a circuit of the block. From an upstairs balcony an old woman in black peers at her suspiciously. It is October; the trees—maples?—are dropping their leaves.

In the entryway she meets the agent, a tall young man in an ill-fitting suit. He shakes her hand; his English, it turns out, is rudimentary.

'Thank you for coming,' she says. 'You understand, I do not want to buy the apartment, I have come only to fetch something. I need no more than a minute of your time.'

He makes no move. Has he understood?

'You open the door for me.' She makes a twisting motion: a key turning in a lock. 'I pick up the box. Then we go. You are a free man. That is all. Okay?'

'Okay,' he says.

There is a problem with the door. The key on his ring, the key that is labelled 2–30—he shows her the label, the number of the apartment—does not fit the keyhole. He shrugs helplessly. *What can I do?* his expression says.

She takes the keyring from him, tries another key. The door opens. 'See?' she says.

She enters, the agent following.

She had expected mahogany furniture, gloom, dust, creaking bookcases, spiders in the corners. In fact, save for a stack of cartons in a corner and four plastic chairs nested into one another, the front room is bare, and—because the curtains have been taken down—flooded with sunlight.

She peers into a minuscule kitchen, into a bathroom with a plastic shower curtain brown with age.

'You are sure this is the correct apartment?' she asks.

The agent shows her the key again, 2–30, the key that does not fit.

It occurs to her that the whole thing may be a trick, a malicious trick: not only not the correct apartment, but also not the correct apartment block, not the correct quarter of the city, perhaps not even the correct house agent. A trick for which only one person can be responsible: the daughter in Berlin, Ewa. Ewa has, out of ill will, sent her off on a pointless errand. *Who is she, this Beatriz? Just another of my father's many girlfriends.*

But she is wrong. No trick. The second room is positively cluttered. It contains a bed (single), two chests of drawers, a rack of men's clothes, an ironing table with a plastic sunflower in a vase, a mirror in an ornate gilt frame, a massive rolltop desk with a formidable typewriter.

There is a third room too, with another kitchen and another bathroom leading off it. This room is bare save for a piano. On one wall is a framed advertisement for a recital at Wigmore Hall, dated 1991, with an image of one of the Pole's younger selves staring abstractedly into the distance. On the piano lid: a picture of young Witold, black and white, unsmiling, receiving some kind of award from a man in a frockcoat; a plaster bust of Johann Sebastian Bach; a more recent picture of Witold, hands clasped, at the centre of a row of women in sparkling evening dress, among whom she recognizes, astonishingly, herself. The Concert Circle sisterhood as it was in 2015, minus Margarita! She has never seen the photograph before. Where did he lay his hands on it?

'See!' she says, pointing.

The house agent peers over her shoulder. 'It is you,' he says.

'Yes,' she says, 'it is me.' Indeed it is! Year after year, unbeknown to her, her image has been casting its faint light over this dreary quarter of this alien city.

But what of the box, the precious box that the elusive Pani Jablońska has prepared for her, the box for whose sake she has crossed half a continent?

The cartons in the front room—there must be twenty of them—have labels scrawled on them that she cannot make out. 'Can you help me?' she says to the young man. 'Can you tell me what these boxes contain?'

The young man takes off his jacket and springs into action. 'This . . . this . . . this—books. All books. Only this . . . this—no books.' He extracts two boxes from the pile. With a kitchen knife she opens them. Men's clothing, smelling of camphor; kitchenware; medicines; odds and ends; nothing for her.

'You look for this?' says the agent. He is holding out a small grey box with a label on it. She reads the label: WITOLD WALCZYKIEWICZ 19.VII.2019. She opens the box. It contains a porcelain urn and the urn contains ash.

'Where did you find it?' she asks.

The agent indicates a shelf in the kitchen.

'Put it back, please.'

She calls Ewa's number, leaves a message: 'Ewa, I am in your father's apartment. I have the house agent with me. We can't find Pani Jabłońska's box. Please call urgently.'

Idly the agent fingers a scale on the piano. He tries to sit down, but the piano stool resists. From its recess he extracts a cardboard box file. On the file is pasted a label with her name and the telephone number of the Sala Mompou.

She opens the file. Loose papers. A binder. A photograph of her, wearing a swimsuit and a wide straw hat, taken years ago, that he must have stolen from the house in Sóller.

'This is it,' she says. 'This is what we have been looking for. Thank you, thank you. I am most grateful. You are free to go now. I will stay behind briefly. I will lock the door behind me when I leave. Is that okay?'

The young man seems dubious. Does he not trust her? She holds out a hand, which after a moment's hesitation he takes. 'Thank you again. Goodbye. *Do widzenia*.' And she watches him leave.

8. She examines the papers: printouts of the handful of emails that passed between the two of them, nothing more. She opens the binder. It contains what are evidently poems, in Polish, one to a page, typewritten and numbered I—LXXXIV.

So this is what Witold W, the less and less famous pianist, has left for her: not music but some kind of manuscript. And this is where he must have been living when he prepared it: in this dreary little apartment in this featureless quarter of the city of his birth. Puzzling. But perhaps this was his notion of a monk's cell, his place of retreat from the world.

She pages through the poems, searching for her name amid the snarl of consonants, and finds it several times—not Beatriz but Beatrice. Thus: a book of Beatrice, put together by an obscure follower of Dante.

9. She could put all this stuff back in the recess of the piano stool and leave it to be carted away to the auction house. Or she could add it to the box of miscellaneous rubbish in the front room, to end its life amid food wrappers and orange rinds and styrofoam in a dump

somewhere in the wasteland of the Polish countryside. She could do that and draw the door closed behind her (*click!*) and call a taxi and get to the airport in time for her late-afternoon flight to Barcelona via Frankfurt and never give another thought to the Pole and his book of Beatrice.

Alternatively, she could take the poems back to Barcelona and get someone to translate them and have them hand-printed on rag paper in a limited edition of ten copies, *El libro de Beatriz* de W.W. One copy for the daughter in Berlin, to prove that she, Beatriz/Beatrice, was no whore, the rest to be stored away in a cupboard for her sons to discover after her death and learn what heights, what depths of passion their mother could inspire, even in her mature years.

What to do? Take the poems with her or leave them here, abandon them, forget about them? The man is dead. The daughter doesn't care. There is no one to answer to but herself.

10. She must read Dante. Her education never took her that far. She knows the picture of him, the famous

picture, but not the poetry. Features not unlike the Pole's. The same scowl.

You should smile more, she told him once. *You have a nice smile. People would warm to you if you could learn to smile.*

11. She too is warming to the Pole, now that she has his testament in her hands. It so happens that she does not go in for grand, hopeless passions—not part of her constitution, evidently—but that does not mean she does not admire grand passions in others. It is pleasing to know that he did not forget her, that far from forgetting her he celebrated her in verse. His Beatrice. It could not have been easy. Even in Spanish getting words to rhyme takes skill. Think of doing it in Polish!

12. She should have a talk with the daughter. On the telephone the daughter came across as cold and inconsiderate, but maybe that was just the ghost of the German language haunting her English. She could drop in on her in her busy-busy restaurant in Berlin. Hello, Ewa,

let me introduce myself. I am Beatriz, the lady friend of your father's from Barcelona. If you have the time, if you are not needed in the kitchen, can we sit down and have a chat? You probably think I am one of those harpies who sink their claws into famous men and suck the blood out of them. Well, you are wrong. I am not like that at all. I did not seek your father's attention. It was he who fell in love with me. I could have slammed the door in his face, but I didn't. I treated him gently, as gently as I could. The memories I left him with were, for the most part, happy. If you do not believe me, take a look: here are the poems he wrote for me.

13. The clock is ticking. It is three in the afternoon. If she wants to sleep in her own bed tonight she must move. Alternatively, she could spend the night in Warsaw, fly out in the morning. She could make herself at home in this apartment, explore the neighbourhood, get a meal somewhere, authentic Polish food (what might that be? blood sausage, boiled potatoes, sauerkraut?), sleep in the dead man's bed. There are practical problems (no electricity, no bedclothes), but they are not insuperable. If the man suffered for her—indeed,

pined for her—does she not owe it to him to suffer a little in return?

14. She leaves a message on her husband's phone: *Staying on in Warsaw. Back tomorrow.*

15. The boys with their bicycles have gone, along with the dog. She makes a tour of the neighbourhood. There is nothing worth seeing, nothing she could not find back home. From a poky little shop (*Supermarket* says the sign) she buys a packet of dried apricots, a packet of biscuits, a bottle of water. She returns to the apartment and, using the last of the daylight, extracts a woollen sweater and a pair of corduroy trousers from the boxes. Her nightwear. The water supply is not cut off, she is able to wash.

16. She sleeps, does not dream. She never dreams. However, during the night she wakes briefly, sensing someone else in the apartment. 'Witold, if that is you, come and lie with me,' she murmurs into the darkness. There is no answering movement, no sound. She goes back to sleep.

17. In the morning she calls for a taxi and by 9 a.m. is at the airport. She has a long wait for her flight; she uses it to have a leisurely breakfast, a massage, a manicure. By 6 p.m. she is home, rested and smiling.

'I got your message,' says her husband. 'How was the trip? Do I need to feel jealous?'

'The man is dead,' she says. 'How can you feel jealous?'

'Alienation of affections,' he says. 'Hasn't he alienated your affections?'

'Don't be ridiculous. I was never in love with him. He was in love with me. A one-sided affair. That's all.'

'And you brought back the box, the famous box? What was in it?'

'There was a misunderstanding. I misunderstood the daughter. I was expecting something personal, but all he left was a book he had published on Chopin, in Polish. As a keepsake. A memento.'

'So it was a waste of time, the whole trip.'

'Not entirely. I got to see Poland, or some of it. I got to see where Witold lived. I got to say goodbye.'

'He was important to you, wasn't he.'

'No, not important, not in himself. But one needs to be reassured every now and again, if one is a woman. One needs proof that one can still make an impression.'

'And I do not provide that proof?'

'Yes, you do. But not enough.'

18. *Not important.* Is she lying? *I was never in love with him.* True. *He was in love with me.* True. Where is the lie in that?

She has secrets from her husband, as he has secrets from her. In a good marriage the partners respect each other's right to have secrets. She has a good marriage; and what passed in Mallorca counts as one of her secrets.

Her husband is a man of the world. He knows how broad a field *We were not lovers* can cover: what it can include, what it excludes. It excludes *My heart belongs to him.* Her heart has never belonged to the Pole.

19. The book about Chopin, the keepsake, is not a fiction. She took it from one of the boxes in the apartment, brought it back so that she could say to her husband, *See: his last gift to me.*

FIVE

1. She calls up a translation program, Polish to Spanish, and types in the first poem of the eighty-four, taking pains to include every single dot and stroke and curlicue. What comes out after she presses the button makes little sense. There are three men in the poem: Homer, Dante Alighieri, and an unnamed vagabond who, with an animal—presumably a dog—at his side, follows in their footsteps, haunting crowded cities and asking people for money. This beggar meets a woman with a beautiful pink birthmark, who brings him peace. After which he finds himself in Warsaw, city of his birth and

death, singing praises of the poet—Homer? Dante?—who showed him the way.

The beggar is clearly the Pole himself, while she, Beatriz, is presumably the woman with the birthmark. But why a birthmark? She has no birthmark. Is the birthmark a symbol of some kind? A symbol of a hidden flaw, perhaps, concealed by her clothing?

She does not demand that the computer provide a perfect translation. All she wants is an answer to the question: Is the tone of the poems positive or negative, celebratory or accusatory? Are they a hymn to the beloved; or on the contrary are they a bitter parting shot from a rejected lover? A simple enough question; but the computer is as tone-deaf as it is stupid.

2. Tomás, her elder son, the one who has always been closer to her, comes to lunch with his wife and child. After lunch she has a chance to speak to him alone. 'You don't happen to know anyone who speaks Polish, do you? I need some translation done.'

'Polish? No, I don't. What exactly do you need translated?'

'It's a long story, Tomás. There was a Polish man, quite a while ago, who was keen on me. He died recently, and his daughter found a suite of poems that he had written, apparently addressed to me, which she has passed on. I'm sure they are not great poetry, but it's sad to think he devoted so much labour to them and no one is ever going to read them. I have tried the computer, but the language is too complicated for it.'

'I'll ask around. I know someone at the university in Vic. They have a unit there that specializes in language teaching. Maybe there is a Polish specialist on the staff. I'll find out. Was he in love with you, this Pole? Who was he?'

'He was a pianist, quite well known. He recorded for DGG. We met when he came to play for the Circle. He had rather unrealistic ideas about me. He wanted me to run away with him to Brazil.'

'He wanted you to give up everything, just like that, and go off with him?'

'Well, he was smitten. I didn't take him seriously. But now there are these poems. I feel a bit guilty. I feel I have a duty to read them. See what you can find. But please don't tell your father. It will only complicate matters.'

3. The next day Tomás calls. Unfortunately they don't teach Polish at Vic. The people there suggest she try the Polish consulate.

On the website of the Polish consulate she finds a brief list of accredited translators. She calls the first on the list: Clara Weisz Urizza, BA (Trieste), Dip.Tr. (Milan). 'I have a text in Polish that I want translated. Can you tell me what you charge?'

'It depends on what kind of text. Is it a legal document?'

'It is a set of poems, eighty-four in total, most of them quite short.'

'Poetry? I am not a literary translator. Normally I translate commercial and legal documents. But send me a sample and I will see what I can do.'

'I would prefer to bring the poems in person. I don't want them to circulate.'

'I have a day job at a travel agency.' She names a travel agency on Las Ramblas. 'You can drop a sample off there.'

'I would prefer to deal with you face to face. If that is not possible, say so, and I will make other arrangements.'

4. On Sunday she takes a taxi to Señora Weisz's address in Gracia. Señora Weisz turns out to be a grey-haired woman with an overflowing bust who speaks rapid Castilian with an Italian accent. The apartment is overheated, nevertheless she wears a sweater.

She offers coffee and too-sweet pastries. 'I confess I have never tried to translate poetry before,' she says. 'I hope it is not too modern.'

She, Beatriz, hands over copies she has made of the first ten poems. 'The author was an acquaintance from Warsaw. He is deceased now. He was not a professional writer. I have no idea of the quality of the verse.'

'What is your desire?' says Señora Weisz. 'Do you want translations that you can publish?'

'No, not at all. We—that is to say, his daughter and I—have no plans for publication. As a first step I would like to get some idea of what the poems say, what they are about.'

Señora Weisz pages through the poems, shaking her head. 'These poems—I can translate the words for you, I can turn Polish words into Spanish words, but I cannot say, "This is what the poem is about, this is what it means." Do you understand what I am saying? Normally

I translate legal documents, contracts. When I translate a contract I must be prepared to swear that the translation is correct. That is what is required from an accredited translator. But interpreting the contract, saying what it means, that is not my job—that is a job for a lawyer. Do I make myself clear? So: I translate your poems for you, and then you decide what they mean.'

'Very well. What will you charge?'

'The charge is seventy-five Euros per hour, that is the standard rate, we are all the same. How many hours? Eighty poems, you say, one page per poem. Maybe ten hours, maybe twenty, maybe more, I cannot say. For me poetry is a new field.'

'Some of the poems are longer than a page, so the page count may be more like a hundred. Can you translate the first poem for me now? Just a rough translation. So that I can get an idea of the tone. I will pay you for the hour.'

'The first poem. It says: The stranger must know that this man has travelled for many years and played the harp in many cities and spoken to animals. The stranger must know that this man—he does not tell the man's name—followed the footsteps of Homer and Dante and stayed in dark forests and crossed the wine-coloured sea. Then the poem says this: He found the perfect rose between the legs of a certain woman, and thus attained final peace. He sings his song in Warsaw, the city where he was born and died, and he sings it in praise of the woman who showed him the way.'

Between the legs of a woman. Nothing about a birthmark. Nothing about a dog. 'That is the end?'

'That is the end.'

'Can you do the second poem too?'

'There is an epigraph: *Per entro i mie' disiri, che ti menavano ad amar lo bene.* The love you felt for me led you to love of the good. That's Dante in old Italian. The poem says this: When he was a dandy, a young man of fashion—you understand?—he liked to look at a particular woman but he could not have her, could not possess her. Her throat is bare, she swings her skirt, something like that. So all the desire, the male desire, climbs up from his private parts, climbs through his blood and his—I would have to look up the correct word in Spanish, it is a medical term—into his eyes. He stares with his eyes and through his eyes he possesses her. Then he goes to a public meeting and he chooses a pretty girl and employs her as a *biombo* or a *pantalla*, it is not clear, some kind of curtain or screen, while with his eyes he eats up the far one, the far woman, whose name is Beatrice, *la modesta* (he uses the Italian word or maybe Spanish, it is the same). Modesty, he says, is her highest virtue, also grace and goodness. Then he says: I had no luck, I came too late, I lived too far away, I had only her picture in my eyes, which is like a bird that flutters in memory. This poem is difficult, much more difficult than the first one, I would have to work on it.'

'Thank you. It is, as you say, a difficult poem. I too don't understand it. Let me pay you, and let me go away and think about it—think whether I want the whole set translated.'

She counts out the fee in notes.

'He says Beatrice,' says Señora Weisz. 'That is not you. That is the girlfriend of the poet Dante.'

'Correct,' she says. 'The Beatrice in the poem has been dead for many years. Whereas I am still alive. Goodbye. I will let you know what I decide.'

Between Señora Weisz and herself there passes something like a smile of complicity.

5. *The love you felt for me led you to love of the good.* He should have written: *The love I felt for you led me to love of*

the good. That would have made it clearer: having parted from his beloved, or been parted, he turned the ache of separation into a project of making himself a better man.

Dante and Beatrice: he was using the wrong myth. Misguided. She is no Beatrice, no saint.

What would have been the right myth? Orpheus and Eurydice? Beauty and the Beast?

6. She turns back to the first poem, the poem that baffled the computer yet spoke so clearly to Señora Weisz. *Homera i Dantego Alighieri* are clearly Homer and Dante, and *idealną różę* must be *una rosa ideal,* an ideal rose. In that case, *wcześniej między nogami jego pani osiągając idealną różę* must be the bit about finding the rose, about attaining transcendence through sexual love; but finding it *between her legs*—what a vulgar way of putting it! No wonder Señora Weisz baulked when she brought out the words. *What am I letting myself in for?* she must have thought to herself. *And is there even worse to come?*

First Pani Jablońska, then the daughter in Berlin—Ewa—and now Señora Weisz. The circle is widening. When Pani Jablońska set aside the manuscript for the mystery woman in Spain, she must surely have sneaked a look at it and been struck by that glaring intimacy on the very first page. And Ewa, despite her denials, must have seen it too. No wonder she was so sniffy on the telephone! How humiliating! How galling!

7. She, Beatriz, comes from a cultivated family. Her grandfather, her father's father, had as a student at the University of Salamanca been witness to a public book-burning and had never forgotten it. *A true act of barbarity*, he called it. In due course he became a professor of law and assembled a considerable library, which after his death went to his eldest son, her uncle Federico. *Burning books is a prelude to burning people*, her grandfather had said, an utterance that became part of the family's folklore. He passed away when she was five years old; she remembers him only as a stout old man with a prickly beard and a cane with an ivory handle.

Burning letters is not the same as burning books. People burn old letters every day of the week. They burn them because they contain nothing of abiding interest or because they have become an embarrassment: letters from childhood sweethearts, for example.

The same holds true, more or less, for diaries. But the Pole's eighty-four poems are not letters except in a certain, unusual sense, nor do they constitute a diary, again except in a certain sense. They constitute a manuscript, that is to say, the embryo of a book. Burning the poems would be more like burning a book than burning old letters. The question is, would burning the poems be an act of barbarity, a prelude to burning people?

The answer is not wholly obvious. In Spain the Pole is a nobody, the record of his love affairs of no interest. Back in Poland, however, he is not a nobody. In Poland there may be a degree of interest, perhaps even a degree of pride, in what a noted interpreter of Poland's national composer has to say about the time he spent between the legs of women. Burning his poems may indeed, to Poles, constitute an act of barbarity. The civilized thing to do would be to return the poems to Poland, to the Chopin Museum or the National Patriotic Library, for their manuscript collection. To return them anonymously, eliminating all trace of herself, so that no one will ever come knocking at the door, now or in the future, saying, 'Are you the original of Beatrice? Are you the woman from Barcelona between whose legs Witold Walczykiewicz had his spiritual revelations?'

8. For days she mulls over the question: Should she burn the poems, or on the contrary should she commission Senõra Weisz to translate them (at no small cost); and, if the latter, is she prepared to read Señora Weisz's translations and thereby submit herself to probable pain and humiliation?

She mulls over the question; then, when the mulling has run its course, gives herself a shake and turns her attention to other things. The folder with the eighty-four poems goes into the bottom drawer of her desk.

Even in the bottom drawer, however, the poems refuse to be forgotten. They burn there with a slow fire.

The Pole wrote the poems to tell her that he went on loving her long after their time together in Mallorca. But he could have achieved the same with a simple letter in the mail: 'My dearest Beatriz, from my deathbed I write to tell you that I loved you to the end. Your faithful servant, Witold.' Therefore, why *poems*? And why so many of them?

The answer can only be: because he wanted not merely to *say* that he loved her but to prove it—prove it by performing for her sake a lengthy and inherently meaningless task. Nonetheless, why poems? If lengthy and meaningless labour is the criterion, why not engrave the Sermon on the Mount on a grain of rice and send it to her in a little plush box?

The answer: because, through his poems, he aspires to speak to her from beyond the grave. He wants to speak to her, to woo her, so that she will love him and keep him alive in her heart.

There are good kinds of love and bad kinds of love. What kind of love is it that burns day and night *between the legs of a woman* in the bottom drawer of her desk?

When she was young she would act on impulse. She followed her impulses because she trusted them. Nowadays she is more prudent. The prudent course of action—no doubt about it—would be to distance herself from the fire, to wait until it had burnt itself out, then, perhaps, if she were still curious, to poke around in the ashes.

9. In Mallorca, in bed with her, he had called it her rose. At the time it felt false, a false word, and now, in his poems, it feels false too. Not a rose in truth, not a flower at all; but what?

She remembers her boys growing up, and their unending curiosity about girls. If girls did not have *it*, what did girls have? It could not be nothing; but if it was not nothing, what could it be? Curiosity; horror too. The two of them in the bath, splashing each other, laughing, raucous, overexcited. *What is* it, *mama!* It: *is that its name?*

It: where they came from, covered in blood and mucus, emerging into the noise and glare of the world. No wonder they wailed—*too much! too much!*—no wonder they clamoured to go back, to curl up in the old familiar nest and suck their thumbs and drowse in peace. And now the Pole, a big man—huge!—but no less babyish, emerging from her body and her bed no less confused, no less frightened. *It*: the rose that is no rose.

10. Boasting. That is how men defend themselves against the confusion. Her sons too, for all she knows, grown men now, men of the world. *I had her, that smart woman from Barcelona. I crushed her in my arms, I crumpled her rose.* The war between men and women, primeval, never-ending. *I had her, she was mine, read all about it.*

She hurt him. She wounded him in his pride. After that insult, all of his labour was self-protective, spinning nacre, layer upon layer of it, over the wound. She invited him into her bed, then she threw him out. His revenge on her: to freeze her, aestheticize her, turn her into an art-object, a Beatrice, a plaster saint to be venerated and carried in procession through the streets. *Mother of mercy.*

11. Yet if he wrote the poems to take revenge on her, how come the epigraph to poem 10, credited to Octavio Paz, whom he quotes in English? *A paradox of love: we love simultaneously a mortal body and an immortal soul. Without the attraction of the body, the lover could not love the soul. To the lover the desired body is a soul.* Was that Witold's story too: that through loving her body he came to love her soul? Fair enough. But it does not answer the question: why *her* body, why *her* soul?

Go back to Beatrice, the real Beatrice. What was it that made Dante choose her over all other women? Or go back to Mary. What was it about Mary full of grace that made God decide to visit her by night? What flexion of the lip, what arch of the eyebrow, what contour of the buttock? At what moment did she, Beatriz, the woman whose job it was to take the visiting soloist out to dinner that fatal evening in 2015, become his destined one? What was it about *her* that brought about her election?

Where was the divine in her, that evening? And where is the divine in her now?

12. Out of the blue, a call from Poland. *Vous parlez français, Madame?* Pani Jablońska, sounding much younger and more spry than she had imagined her to be. Apologies for not responding earlier, but there had been a crisis in the family, she had had to go to Łodz in a hurry, in fact she is still in Łodz. Apologies for not being able to open the apartment, apologies for missing her visit, did she recover all the materials Witold left for her? Dear Witold, so sorely missed. And Ewa, always so busy, and now having to arrange everything from a distance: so inconvenient, such a pity!

She, Beatriz, is in no mood to listen to a torrent of words in an unfamiliar language (*un peu plus lentement, s'il vous plaît!*), but there are things she would like to know, things that only the Polish neighbour can tell her. Such as, for instance: what has been the fate of the apartment where she spent her solitary Polish night, an abode still haunted (if her experience counts) by the ghost of its master? Such as: aside from the poems, is she, Pani Jablońska, in possession of any supplementary message meant for her, Beatriz, the lady from Barcelona? Such as (if she can bring herself to ask): did the late lamented Witold ever show her his poems, in particular the first poem, with its metaphoric use of the word *rose*?

You must know, continues Pani Jablońska, that Witold owned not one but two apartments in the block—two adjacent apartments—and put in a communicating door—this was back in the 1990s, when everything was going cheap—but that unfortunately it was done without the proper paperwork, builders did things *à l'arabe* in those days, and now the apartment that is in fact two apartments with two postal addresses cannot be sold until the paperwork is regularized, which Ewa, poor Ewa, is having to do from Germany. Ewa got people to come with a truck and clear it out, the furniture, the books, everything, including Witold's piano, so at the moment it is standing empty, yet it can't be put on the market, such a tragedy.

À l'arabe: what can that mean? Or did she mishear?

'If I may interrupt,' she says, 'did Witold happen to say anything about me?'

There is a long, long silence. For the first time it occurs to her that the story of a sudden dash to Łodz may be fabricated, that Pani Jablońska may be not at all the wizened little old Polish widow dressed in black whom she has pictured to herself, that the very phrase *Witold's neighbour* may itself be a delicate euphemism not unconnected with the talk of a double apartment with a communicating door.

'If he didn't have anything to say, it doesn't matter,' she says, breaking the silence. 'Thank you for getting in touch. It is very kind of you.'

'Wait,' says Pani Jabłonska. 'Is there nothing else you would like to know?'

'About Witold? No, Madame, I don't think so. I know all that I need to know.'

13. *Is there nothing else?* What was the woman threatening to tell? How poor Witold suffered? How he faced his death? No, she would prefer it if that were left in decent obscurity.

If she opens the gate a crack, who knows what might not come pouring through?

14. She calls Señora Weisz. 'I have decided that you should translate all the poems, from beginning to end.

I will send the full set via courier to the travel agency, addressed to you, marked Personal. I don't want anyone else to see them. Can I rely on you?'

'You can rely on me. Poetry is not my strong point, but I will do my best. Perhaps you can make a down payment.'

'I will enclose a cheque with the file. Shall we say five hundred?'

'Five hundred would be good.'

15. After a week, a message from Señora Weisz. The translations are done. The bill comes to fifteen hundred Euros.

I will drop by and fetch the translations this evening, she replies.

The door is opened by a young man. 'Hi. You are the lady for the poems? Come in. I am Natán. My mother isn't home yet, but she won't be long. Please sit down. Do you want to see the poems?' He passes her a bulky packet: her photocopies plus the Spanish translations neatly printed out. She glances at the first one. *The lady between whose legs* is still there.

'I helped her now and again,' says Natán. 'Poetry isn't really my mother's thing.'

'You speak Polish too?'

'Not really. But I have read lots of Polish poetry. In Poland poetry is a disease, everyone catches it. Your poet—what is his name?'

'Walczykiewicz. Witold Walczykiewicz. He died not long ago. Have you been to Poland?'

'Poland is shit. Who would want to go there? It used to be bad. Now it's even worse.'

It dawns on her that they are Jews, Clara and her son, with good and sufficient reason not to like Poland.

'Walczykiewicz.' He pronounces the name like a native, better than she does, she between whose legs its bearer has lain. 'He is not a great poet, is he?'

'Poetry wasn't his medium. He was really a musician, a pianist. He was well known as an interpreter of Chopin.'

'The poems are pretty average, but there are a few that stand out. Are they about you?'

She is silent.

'He was in love with you, I would bet. If he knew you couldn't read Polish, why didn't he translate them for you?'

'Polish was his mother tongue. You can only write poetry in your mother tongue. At least that is what I was taught. Maybe it didn't matter to him that I couldn't read his poems. Maybe the important thing was to express himself.'

'Maybe. What I like best about them is that they aren't dry and ironic like everyone else's. Do you know Cyprian Norwid? No? You should read him. Walczykie-wicz is like Cyprian Norwid, only not in the same class. His best poem—you will see it—is the one where he dives down to the seabed and finds himself face to face with a marble statue, and realizes it is Aphrodite—you know, the goddess. She has big painted eyes that look through him without seeing him. Eerie. I read some-where that the Mediterranean is full of stuff from old shipwrecks—coins, statues, crockery, wine jars. I would like to go diving off the Greek coast sometime—who knows, I might be lucky.'

'Witold wasn't lucky.'

The boy looks at her oddly.

'I mean, he wasn't a lucky person. If he had gone div-ing he wouldn't have found a goddess. He would have come up empty-handed. Or he would have drowned. That's the way he was. What are you studying?'

'Economics. It isn't my thing, as my mother would say, but nowadays one has to. To get on.'

'I have two sons, a bit older than you. They didn't

study economics but they have got on pretty well. They have made successes of their lives.'

'What did they study?'

'One studied biochemistry, the other studied engineering.'

There is more that she could say about her sons, much more, but she does not. She is proud of her sons, of the way in which they assumed responsibility for their lives early on, as though their lives were business enterprises that needed to be managed firmly and wisely. They take after their father, both of them. Neither takes after her.

'What are you going to do with the poems?' the boy asks. 'Will you be publishing them?'

'I don't think so. If they are not very good, as you say—and I am sure you are right—who would want to buy them? No, I won't publish them, but I did promise Witold before he died that I would take care of them, look after them. I can't find a better way to say it.'

Clara Weisz arrives, her arms full of packages. 'I'm sorry I'm late. Has Natán shown you the poems? I hope you like them. It wasn't as hard as I had feared, once we got going. An interesting man, Walczykiewicz. I looked him up on the Internet. As you say, he was a pianist, but did he tell you that when he was a young man, back in the 1960s, he published a book of verse? What we call a *publikacja ulotna*, a fleeting publication or fugitive publication. He wasn't popular with the authorities of the day.'

'I don't know much about his early life. He wasn't a very communicative man.'

'Well, it's all in the Polish Wikipedia, if you can read Polish.'

'Let me write you a cheque. You said fifteen hundred, less the advance?'

'That's correct. One thousand. I translated the hand-written notes too, but on separate pages. You will see.'

'Oh. I thought the handwritten bits were part of the poems—revisions, additions, that sort of thing.'

'No, I don't think so. But you can decide for yourself.'

She takes her leave. They will not see each other again, she and the Weiszes. A relief. They know too much about her. Yet what does it amount to, what they know? That she had an affair with a man? It happens every day. That the man was left heartbroken and wrote poems about her? That too happens, though not every day. No, the shame is that Clara Weisz, who is no one to her and no one to Witold, has had access to what was going on in Witold's soul, clearer access than she, for whom the poems were written, will ever have, given that there must be tones, echoes, nuances, subtleties in the Polish that no translation can ever transmit. Without the slightest effort Clara Weisz has become the Pole's first, best reader, with her son in second place, while she comes limping behind, a poor third.

16. She reads Clara's handiwork through from beginning to end, rapidly. Not all the poems are comprehensible, though the prose versions are remarkably lucid. But by the end she has an answer to her overriding question. The poems are not an act of revenge, not at all. They are, in the broadest sense, a record of love.

She rereads a block of poems towards the end in which the phrases 'the other world' and 'the next life' come up repeatedly. The poems must date from when the Pole was facing death and trying to convince himself it was not the end of everything.

She tries to imagine what deus ex machina he could have thought would extract him from his present world, a world of loss and woe, and install him in the next one. As far as she can see, transport would be achieved in an instant, more or less magically. He would arrive in the next world a fully formed adult with an adult's bagful of memories and longings, to begin preparing for the day when she too will arrive, his Beatrice, to set up house with him in holy matrimony. She shivers. He cannot wait to see her again, but does she care to see him? The truth is that by the time the daughter phoned to announce his death she had all but forgotten him, or at least moved him into the no-longer-active bin.

Mourning is a natural process. All the peoples of the planet have rituals of mourning. Even elephants. She, Beatriz, lost her mother early. The loss left a gaping hole in her life. She grieved, she mourned, she missed her. Then at a certain point the mourning came to an end and she moved on. But the Pole does not seem to have moved on. Having lost her, he mourned her and went on mourning, nursing his loss like a mother who refuses to give up a dead child.

He *says* he expects to be reunited with her in the next world, but what can that possibly mean? There must have been moments when, sitting alone in his dreary apartment in Warsaw, he knew he had seen the last of her. To make that real-life loss bearable he must have thrown all his failing powers into invoking, creating, calling into being a *new* Beatriz, a transfigured yet substantial version of herself, who, far from dismissing him and—even worse—forgetting him, was by secret, mystical means urging him to prepare a celestial home for her.

She does not believe in life after death, except in the most metaphorical of senses. When she is dead her children will remember her and reminisce about her, fondly or not so fondly. They might also pick her to pieces with their psychoanalysts (*Was she a good mother? Was she a bad mother?*). As long as they go on doing so she will enjoy a flickering kind of life. But with the passing of their generation she will be tossed into a dusty archive, there to be shut out from the light of day for ever and ever. Such constitutes her belief, her mature, adult belief; and she does the Pole the credit of accepting that, when he was not absorbed in his music and his poetry, he shared it too—that he did not *really* believe there would be another life in another world where the two of them would find each other and enjoy the happiness that chance had withheld from them in their first incarnation.

So why write—and commit to her—these poems from his last months in which he looks forward so confidently to seeing her again, poems that steadfastly avoid the questions that dog any theory of the afterlife? Questions such as: Will the beloved not arrive attended by a host of spouses and lovers all looking forward to spending the afterlife by her side and in her bed? Will there be no jealousy in the afterlife? No boredom? No hunger? No bowel movements? What about clothes? Will we all have to wear shapeless smocks down to our ankles? And underwear—will a touch of lace be permitted or will everything have to be very plain, very puritan?

Heaven: a vast ante-room full of souls milling about in their uniform smocks, searching anxiously for their other halves.

17. It is not entirely true that he dodges the question of physical appearance. In one of his afterworld poems he writes that he and she will meet naked, and then confesses that in the present world—he must be referring to Mallorca—it was a matter of shame to him that he could bring to the table of love nothing but his ugly old male body.

18. Why is she so hard on him? Why does she hover over his poetic legacy with a scalpel at the ready? Answer:

because she was hoping for more. It is hard to admit to, but she was hoping that the man who loved her would have used that love, that energy, that *eros*, to bring her to life better than he has managed to do. Vanity on her part? Yes, perhaps. But the Pole thought of himself as an artist in the grand old sense, a *maestro*, and an artist in the grand old sense (Dante!) would have given her a new life that was believable, that was proof against her own easy mockery. *For the lover the desired body is a soul.* The Pole loved her body. The Pole loves her soul (so he says). But where in the poems does she see body transfigured into soul?

Señora Weisz's son thought the poems weak, and in most cases she agrees. Did the Pole see their weakness too? Did he see it, yet proceed nevertheless with his scribbling, keeping himself busy so that he would not have to see death sidling up to him?

With the whole of his pathetic project laid out before her on her desk, his project of resurrecting and perfecting a love that was never firmly founded, she is overcome with exasperation but also with pity. The picture grows clearer and clearer before her eyes: the old man at his typewriter in his ugly apartment, trying to force into life his dream of love, using an art that he was not master of.

I should never have encouraged him, she thinks. *I should have nipped the whole thing in the bud. But I did not see where it was leading. I did not see it was going to end up like this.*

She puts the translations back in their folder. Who else but she would ever want to read this stuff? All for nothing, all that patient labour, all that packing of one brick on top of another. There is not even a museum of bad poetry where it can be stored away, along with the rest of the lifeless verbiage that emerges from the hands of men like him, men who lack the art that quickens the word. *Poor old fellow!* she thinks. *Poor old guy!*

19. Did it occur to him that they might fail to meet in the afterlife not because there is no afterlife but because fate will have consigned him to the basement realm while she floats above in Paradise, eternally unattainable?

20. Or the reverse?

SIX

Dear Witold,

Thank you for the book of poems. You won't believe what a roundabout road they have taken, but at last they have arrived in a version I can read.

Natán, the son of my translator, a nice young man, though a bit forward, told me he liked the Aphrodite poem best, the one in which you sink to the bottom of the sea and meet Aphrodite in the form of a marble statue.

If Aphrodite is supposed to stand for me, if I am supposed to be Aphrodite, you have made a mistake. I am not that particular goddess. In fact I am not a goddess at all.

Ditto if I am supposed to be Beatrice.

You complain that the undersea Aphrodite looked straight through you without noticing you. For my part, I thought I saw you pretty well—saw you for what you were and accepted you. But perhaps you wanted more. Perhaps you wanted me to see a god in you, which I never did. My apologies.

A poem that touched me particularly was the one about yourself as a little boy receiving a lesson in anatomy from your mother. During all the time I knew you, I confess, I never once thought of you as a little boy. I treated you as a rational grown-up and expected you to treat me in the same way. That may have been another mistake. If we had dropped the adult masks and approached each other as child to child we might have done better. But of course, becoming a child is not as easy as it looks.

You made one or two proposals to me that I found disconcerting—for example that I run away with you to Brazil—but you never actually wooed me. Nor in the end did you seduce me. No seduction took place, as I think you will agree.

I would have liked to be wooed. I would have liked to be seduced. I would have liked to have been paid the sweet compliments and told the flattering lies that men tell the women they want to sleep with. Why? I don't know and don't care to know. A womanly longing, forgivable.

Why did you obey so meekly when I told you to leave and go back to Valldemossa? Why did you not bombard me with pleas? *I cannot live without you!*—why did you never utter those words?

Theatrics, Witold—have you never heard of theatrics? Listen to Chopin. Listen to the Ballades. Forget about your own tight little readings. Open your ears, for a change, to the real Chopin performers, the enthusiasts who revel in the theatrics of his music and don't mind hitting a wrong key now and then.

And why did you not write to me, or call me, when you knew you were dying? It would have been so easy—so much easier than writing poems. Your neighbour says you did nothing in your last years but labour on your poems. She says you gave up music. Why? Did you lose faith?

If you were Dante, I would go down in history

as your inspiration, your Muse. But you are not Dante. The evidence is before us. You are not a great poet. No one is going to want to read about your love for me, and—on mature consideration—I am glad about that, glad and relieved. I never asked to be written about, by you or by anyone else.

In case you have forgotten it, here is the poem I was referring to, in its new Spanish guise (no rhymes).

POEM 20

'Have *you* got one?' I asked my mother
as she dried me after my bath.
'No,' said my mother, 'I am the woman,
the one built to receive,
while you, my young man,
are the one built to give.
Your pipi is for giving—never forget that.'
'Give what, Mama?'
'Give joy. Give illumination. Give seed
so that again and again

season after season
the new crop will burst forth.'

Give seed—what did that mean?
I saw only darkly
As for *illumination*
I saw it not at all
not until she came to shine her light on my path
Beatrice.

Yet what did I give her
entering her body
the body of all women
the body of the goddess?
dead seed or no seed
no joy
no light

Courage, said Mama.
Like the serpent swallowing its tail
time has no end.
Always there is a new time
a new life
una vita nuova.

But now
my little prince
it is time for bed.

A nice poem, I am sure you will agree.

Yours,
Beatriz

Dear Witold,

A second letter. Don't worry, there won't be too
many. I don't want to turn you into my secret friend,
my phantom companion, my phantom limb.

To begin with, apologies for yesterday's rant.
I don't know what got into me. You may not be
Dante but your poems mean a great deal to me.
Thank you for them.

I am writing to say I hope you didn't have too
painful an end. When I visited the apartment in
Warsaw I came across your ashes in a jar. Your
daughter had forgotten to take them, or else they

were delivered too late, after she had gone back to Berlin. The neglect of your remains strikes me as a bit casual, even by contemporary standards, if you don't mind my saying so. Surely there is a Heroes' Acre in Warsaw, or something like it, where you could be fittingly interred.

Both your daughter and your friend Madame Jabłońska, who when I last heard was in Łodz visiting her family, have been discreet about the manner of your passing.

I raise the matter because of the handwritten words in the margin of the second-last poem, poem 83. I took the words to be part of the poem, but my translator disagrees. She points out that they don't fit anywhere, and furthermore are in neither Polish nor Italian but English. She calls them 'extra-poetic.' The words in question are: 'Save me, my Beatrice.'

If the words belong in the poem and 'Beatrice' is the heavenly being you have adopted from your friend and mentor Dante, well and good, I say no more. But if Beatrice is me, and if when you wrote those words you were pleading with me to save you—to come and save you from death—I must tell you, first, that the message did not reach me, telepathically or otherwise, and, second, that even if it had reached me I would probably not have come. I would not have come to you in Warsaw just as I would not run away with you to Brazil. I was fond of you (let me use that word), but not so extravagantly fond that I would have given up everything for you. You were in love with me—I have no doubt about that—and love is by nature extravagant. As for me, however, my feelings were more shaded, more complex.

That may seem a heartless thing to say at a time when you are defenceless, but it is not so intended. You had the whole creaking philosophical edifice of romantic love behind you, into which you slotted me as your *donna* and saviour. I had no such resources, apart from what I regard as a saving scepticism about schemes of thought that crush and annihilate living beings.

We can be honest with each other—can't we?—now that you are dead. What would be the point of pretending? Let us resolve to be honest yet never cruel.

In a spirit of honesty, I am not going to pretend that I like the very first poem in the series, and the coarse way in which you describe our physical relations. I suspect that your daughter got to see the poem, and that it coloured her attitude towards me. She treated me as if I were your whore.

Nor am I impressed by the second poem. I don't in general like men who stare at women. I don't find being stared at seductive—not in the slightest. And what is *chyme* (the translator's word)? The dictionary says it is a bodily fluid, but what is the sense of it?

POEM 2

Above all he craved to look on her,
he the old master, then a young buck.
Because he could not have her
(bared throat, flurry of skirts, unimaginable)
all the erotic charge ascended from his loins,
ascended through the blood, through the chyme,
to suffuse his living gaze.
Staring at her was his way of possessing her.
In public gatherings he would choose at random
    some attractive girl
set her in his line of sight, seem to be sending her looks

(he called her his screen)

while secretly it was the farther one he was devouring,

his Beatrice

his quarry

la modesta, the modest one.

(Modesty high among her virtues:

modesty, grace, goodness.)

As for me, I had no luck,

came too late, lived too far away

had only her image to close my eyes on

poor fluttering little thing in the chambers of memory.

I find it a difficult poem—too difficult for me. I hope the translation does justice to it. You will be the best judge. The translator was not a professional.

La modesta. Thank you for that. Thank you for your high opinion of me. I will try to live up to it.

But it is getting late. Good night, my prince—time for bed. Sleep well. Sweet dreams.

Yours,
Beatriz

P.S. I will write again.